NINE

TALES

A collection of stories by Forrest A. Abell

American Literary Press, Inc.
Five Star Special Edition
Baltimore, Maryland

NINE TALES

Library of Congress
Cataloging in Publication Data
ISBN 1-56167-344-7

Library of Congress Card Catalog Number:
96-071909

Published by

American Literary Press, Inc.
Five Star Special Edition
8019 Belair Road, Suite 10
Baltimore, Maryland 21236

Manufactured in the United States of America

Table of Contents

Monster the Cat

Monster is a strange name for a cat. How could anyone name a cat monster? The answer is revealed later in this story.

When Monster was a kitten, the cruel lady across the street from our house divorced her husband, sold the house and moved. She left the two little kittens on the back porch, to live or die. She was so heartless she did not care what happened to them. The kittens had no choice but to go into the nearby woods for shelter and an opportunity to forage for food.

Our house was located at the edge of the woods, and from time to time I would see the cats, now quite well grown. I did not pay too much attention to them because a lot of animals roamed those woods. In fact the woods were the Great Swamp located in New Jersey containing about fifteen hundred acres of tall trees, several fruit bearing bushes and swamp brush.

The herd of fourteen deer would visit my back yard and eat honeysuckles off the garden fence. They were very tame, but they knew my every move. I could back out of the garage, make the turn and go up the driveway. If I stopped for any reason they would run away. The same applied when I came home. I would put the auto into the garage, close the overhead door, walk up the stairs to the back door and they would act as if I was not there. If I deviated to the smallest degree, they were off and running. I didn't bother them and they didn't bother me, except when they tried to get into my vegetable garden. Their delicacy was green tomatoes, they would defy me to get to them. I had to put up a nine foot wire fence to keep them out. At the end of the season, I would open the gate and let them have a good meal, which they relished while they kept an eye on me.

During the month of October, I noticed one of the cats, a Seal Point Siamese, sitting in the small basement window. She was enjoying the heat from the furnace and was well protected from the wind and rain. The window faced the East and there was considerable time during which she could have warmth and shelter.

I tried to befriend her, to no avail. When I got too close she would run into the woods. She defiantly did not trust anyone. I learned later that someone had shot her with a pellet and she was blind in one eye. I decided to tame her, but how? When I got near she ran away. In fact, she could sense the breach of her security almost before I moved. She was a learned survivor. I knew it would be a real challenge to get to be her friend, but the odds were in my favor. I had the food and winter was fast approaching.

I decided that the aroma of food would be a good way to get her hungry. I fried some ham and sneaked along the inside wall of the basement where she could not see me. I was able to get the food within inches of her, and she was so interested she pushed against the window screen. She meowed, I suppose because the food tantalized her smell buds. The next evening, I repeated the temptation. She must have been confused and she tried in vain to see from where the food aroma was coming. She meowed and pressed harder against the screen, then she turned the corner of the house and tried to determine where the food was.

After a few sessions of getting her very hungry, I put some food at a place she would have to pass on the way back to her woods.

I played this game for a few days and switched from ham to tuna. Almost every day she came to the window and looked for the food. She would eat and return to her place of safety, her woods.

I talked to her from a distance and let her see me putting

the food out for her. One day I gave her a saucer of warm milk. She drank it with gusto. I found out later that she hated milk. It is very unusual for a cat not to like milk.

Weeks later, after my feeding her and talking to her, she came over to the eating place while I was near. I got tired of playing games, so I decided to play a trick on her. I took the food out to the usual place, talked to her and took the food with me around the house to the basement door. She was reluctant to follow me in a situation like this, but I had her dinner. She had to decide what to do. She thought about it for a short time, I talked to her, and she followed me to the basement door. But she stopped right there. She didn't like the looks of a place with only one way out. Smart cat. I was smarter. I put the food just inside the doorway, and went out of sight. She ate and went to her retreat for the night.

I was making progress. At this point, I felt the score was about sixty/forty in my favor. My ego was probably the reason for my continuing the cat and man game. The cat was still the deciding factor on how far and how fast the game would be played. That must have satisfied her ego, and believe me, she had one.

Time was in my favor; the weather was turning much colder. Finally, the snow came and I decided to play dirty pool. I put the storm window into the basement window. That stopped the heat from passing through. It was warm only when the sun was shining and only during the morning. As soon as the sun passed, no heat. I left my auto out beside the garage and she got onto the hood and slept while the heat lasted, then it was back to the woods for her.

At last, a rainy, cold blizzard came. I prepared a dish of warm food and put it at the open basement door. While she was eating, I slowly closed the door using string I had attached to it. She tried to get out, but it was no use. I expected her to panic, but she ran from one side of the basement floor to the other. She jumped up onto the window sill, but of course, there was no way she could get through

5

it. I sat in the middle of the floor and talked to her for a while. After we spent time trying to figure out each other, she jumped up onto a big cloth covered chair and laid down. I just said good night to her, went up the stairs and left her alone for the night.

In my ambition to trap her, it didn't occur to me to have a litter box for her. I went through the outside garage door and put a full box of earth beside the auto. Then I opened the inside door to the garage, went out through the overhead door and went to bed. I knew if she had to go, she would look for a way out and find the litter box. I suppose she felt trapped because she didn't use it or dirty the basement.

The next morning, I took her breakfast down and she came over and ate it. I reached over and stroked her. She flinched, but let me stroke her a few more times. SUCCESS!!! I opened the door and she ran into her woods.

When I got home from work, she was waiting for her dinner. I left the auto out so she could get warm and prepared tuna for her. I opened the basement door and she followed me. She ate and I petted her, then she just plain ignored me. I wondered what she would do. She surprised me, she decided not to go into the cold woods. She jumped up onto the big chair and decided that would be just fine for the night. I petted her a few strokes and went my way.

The next day, she ate her breakfast, took a look out the door at the snow and sleet and decided the big chair would suit her needs while she waited for dinner. She now accepted me as her friend and knew that she could trust me.

That evening after dinner, she followed me up the stairs to explore the house. She spent about an hour sniffing everything. She selected a place to sleep in back of the sofa. It was carpeted and very cozy. I made a fire in the fireplace, which scared her, but she soon felt the heat and laid on the hearth. I watched her because she was getting very hot. I thought she might burn herself, it was all so new to her.

I turned the television on and she ran into another room.

She didn't like the sound of other people talking. After a while, with the curiosity of a cat, she ventured back into the room. I got the surprise of my life, she sat on the floor in front of my chair and all of a sudden, she jumped onto my lap and laid down and started to purr. I petted her and she went to sleep. When I had to get up to go to bed, the Siamese attitude came through, loud and clear, she objected to being disturbed.

We became good friends, in fact, so good that she started bossing me around. Within a week or two, she even let me have a little space, provided it pleased her.

I had a drop leaf table in the living room by the thermopane picture window, with an eastern exposure. She claimed that for her daytime sitting place. She could see everything that was going on and watch for me to come home. It must have pleased her to sit there and look out at the snow and be so warm. All was peaceful until one stormy evening a friend of hers came to the door looking for food. Monster was not too happy about his showing up and considered him trouble. However, she made a concession and let him enjoy dinner. He decided to take a look around to see where he could sleep for the night. He, too, selected the floor in back of the sofa. That upset Monster, she tolerated his coming to dinner, but wanted "no overnight stays." The visitor had to go and she meant it. She actually growled at him. I opened the door and Fluffy went out to find a place to get out of the weather. It was no hardship for him, he had thick fur that would keep him warm in any kind of weather. Peace and order had been restored in Monster's house.

Springtime came and the ground moles started to dig tunnels through my front yard. They were quite a nuisance. Everything that I tried to get rid of them failed. One day, I looked out the window to see what Monster was up to. She was having fun catching ground moles. Catching them, for her, was easy. She would put her paw down into the tunnel and wait for them to back right into her sharp claws, then she would pull them up and bring them onto the back porch to show me what a good hunter she was.

Monster would challenge me to the "nth" degree. One day, I gave her an off brand tuna, she refused to eat it. She refused, I insisted. I told her she had to eat it. I said she would not get anything else until she ate it. She proceeded to take her paw and cover it up with the newspaper. She knew how to express her feelings. I said to her, "You Brat, you are determined to have your way, but you are an adorable animal."

I married a very nice girl that had three children and a mutt dog. Monster hated riding in an auto. I had to put her into a clothes basket and tie a cover on it. She clawed and chewed at the basket. She was one scared animal, of course, she did not know what was taking place. I tried to assure her everything was all right, but she would not accept it. We got her into the garage at the new home and let her out of the basket. She went berserk, she was uncontrollable.

I just had to let her wear herself out. Then I picked her up and held her on my lap. That settled her down for a while. I felt so sorry for her. Her whole world had been taken away and she was in a strange house with other people.

The mutt dog decided to keep Monster in a corner of a bedroom upstairs and would not let her come down until about four-thirty in the afternoon. Then, sometimes, the dog would chase Monster around the house until Monster would stand her ground and claw the dog until she bled.

The dog died a couple of months later and Monster realized that everyone in the house adored her and she settled down. However, whenever anybody did anything that did not please her, she would wait at the door to tell me all about it. She would look at that person and growl. If my wife did not cut the chicken just right, she would complain.

One evening, the neighbor's big black cat dared to come into Monster's back yard. Monster attacked the cat and both cats got cut up a bit. Monster had to be taken to the veterinarian to have a tooth pulled that had been broken and get a few stitches in her face.

Monster still would not concede one inch of her domain. One day the neighbor's small poodle dared to come onto her porch. The poodle encountered Monster, she clawed a lot of hair off the dog and sent him flying back home. He didn't try that again.

I did not have her declawed because she was blind in one eye and needed all the defense she could have.

Oh! I almost forgot to tell you why I named her Monster. One day, a stranger came into the house. He reached out to pet her, I don't know why she took an immediate disliking to him, but she reared up on her hind legs and went after him with both front paws, claws extended, and scratched him severely. I had to pull her away and hold her. I cannot figure why she attached him, unless she thought he looked like the person that shot her in the eye. My theory might have been true because she had never attacked anyone before.

Age was catching up with her. I would put her on a hassock, in a big chair where the sun could keep her warm, until I came home and fed her and carried her to her litter box. Then I would hold her until bedtime before I put her into a basket filled with soft material.

She got so feeble she could not walk and one day she laid down on the floor, gave a big breath and expired. She was seventeen years old.

I wrapped her in a towel, put her into a steel box with a lock on it and buried her in her woods, her refuge. My house was only two miles from the woods, but that trip seemed to take forever.

Teenagers' Justice

The year was 1930 and I was a boy of sixteen. We were living in a small country mountain top town of about two hundred people. It was a beautiful place, with farm fields, endless mountain scenes, pine trees, a small stream flowing through the town. It was a real fairyland in the springtime, serene.

The down side was that it was the time of the Great Financial Depression. Poverty was playing havoc with the lives of people. We didn't feel the effects of the depression because we had very little under normal circumstances. Finding employment was almost impossible, except for summer farm work. There were no vocational or technical schools to attend where one might learn a trade.

I was lucky, I noticed an advertisement in the local paper for a farm hand at two dollars a day and three farmhouse meals. The farmer interviewed me, and I was pleased to get the job. It was hard work from seven in the morning until six in the evening. The problem was I had to walk three miles to and from work. Sometimes, I could hitch a ride in the morning, but it seemed that few people used that road in the evening. Most of the trip was down a slight grade, however.

After a few weeks, the getting to and from work was getting to be too much for me. I told the farmer that I was resigning for that reason. He said if I stayed on the job I could sleep at the farmhouse. I was quick to accept his offer. I could sleep until six o'clock and go to bed early in the evening. He assigned me a room down stairs, which had a private lavatory. Gosh! I had it made. There was a river nearby and I would take baths there.

The farmer had a friend that would bring his wife and two very well behaved children to visit him and his wife, sometimes once a week. I believed that the farmer and his friend were into some sort of illegal business because the visitor had an auto and was always well dressed, so were his wife and children. It seemed like he did not have a job because he showed up any day of the week. Sometimes the guests would stay overnight, have breakfast and go on their way. The farmer and his friend never talked much in the presence of anyone.

I found out later why. The farmer was making moonshine whiskey, rustling cattle and anything else he could do to make money. Most of the farmers in the area were struggling to make a living, but this farmer was not having any obvious financial problems. He had the best horses and best farm equipment. He was also generous to his wife and friends. He had just bought a new Model A Ford auto, while most farmers had a horse and buggy.

All went well until one morning when I heard a lot of commotion and loud talking upstairs. The farm lady came down and prepared my breakfast—those mouth watering sour cream and buttermilk pancakes, sometimes with bacon and sometimes with homemade country smoked sausage.

While I was eating, the farmer's guest and family came downstairs and seated themselves at the table. The farmer came downstairs in a big hurry, burst into the kitchen and announced that someone had stolen his wife's wedding ring. He demanded that whoever had it surrender it to him this minute. He said no one was to leave the room until he had the ring.

I immediately declared my innocence and offered to let him search me and my room. He said it was not the monetary value of the ring, but the fact that it was near and dear to him. He just raved on and on and kept threatening us. I said I was sorry that I had become the victim of such circumstances. We all tried to calm him, but to no avail. He was a raving, out of control person. Finally, he threatened bodily harm to us. I took a stand and told him I was innocent, and if he approached me, I would have no alternative but to defend myself, even to kill him if necessary.

I believed that was the turning point for his out of control attitude. He calmed down, but demanded the return of the ring and realized we might have to kill him to save ourselves. He said, "The person that stole the ring would regret it." He sat at the table and stared at the ceiling like he was wondering what to do.

I stood up and said, "I have work to do." Then I went out, harnessed the horses and went into the field. I decided to resign and get out of there, but I thought if I did, that would point the finger of guilt toward me. Also, there were only a few weeks left in the term of my employment, so I decided to stay on the job.

While we were eating lunch, the farmer's wife came into the kitchen and said she had found her ring. She had transferred it to another night gown while she was laundering the other one and had forgotten where she had put it. Everyone was relieved and she was smiling because she had recovered the ring.

I got up from the table halfway through the meal, and said, "I am resigning as of this minute, before I become another suspect in a violent situation."

The farmer apologized and begged me to forgive his maniac behavior. He said it would not happen again. I decided to stay because, of all things, I had an eating habit that would change if I went home. My parents didn't need another freeloader.

The farmer expressed quite a liking towards me. One Saturday evening, I decided to walk into town, which was about a two mile trek, and there was a light rain. SURPRISE! The farmer said he was not going to use his auto and handed me the keys to it. He said to be careful and enjoy it. The first thought that ran through my mind was, "Wait till my friends see me driving a new Ford with wire spoke wheels and all shined up." I was floating on air—or was it my ego?

Anyway, I was pleased that the farmer trusted me. In fact, that was the first time he really did anything out of the ordinary for me. He would assign the work he wanted done, I would do it and we would have very little conversation. I spent most of my evenings in my room listening to my radio, or in the club house, as we called it. It was a shanty with a pot belly stove in it and we would take shelter from the inclement weather and use it on weekends for a place to play checkers or cards, tell stories and repeat jokes that we had heard.

All was friendly and quiet until one day when I remarked that the farm work and farm food were doing me a lot of good. I told a group of visitors that I would lift the two rear wheels of the ice wagon off the barn floor. The farmer never missed an opportunity to challenge someone to take a gambling bet. He said he would bet me a month's monetary wages that I could not do it. He said, "Do you know what that wagon weighs?" I said, "No, but I can lift it." I said, "This is a good time to settle the bet. There are plenty of witnesses here, let's go."

We went to the barn, I put my back under the rear portion of the wagon, lifted it about three inches off the floor, and let it drop with a bang to make sure everyone knew that I had lifted it. I held out my palm and said to the farmer, "You lost, pay me." He said, "You don't think I am going to give you sixty dollars, do you?" I said, "Yes I do, you are not giving me sixty dollars, you are settling a bet." He said he was only joking. I said, "Sir, we had a bet, you lost. You will pay me now or you will pay me later." He didn't look scared. I was on his property, in his employ and a youngster. The witnesses just said nothing and went on their way. I suppose they could not believe he would welsh on the bet. I am confident, if I lost, he would not have paid me the last month's salary. I could do nothing about it, so I forgot it.

When I went back to school, I told some of my classmates about what he had done. They were furious because some of them had heard of his wrong doings. One of the boys said we would fix him, real good. We all knew he was making moonshine whiskey and selling it to a club in town. He would put the whiskey into a hollow tree down by the mill stream. The club owner would pick up the whiskey and put the money into the tree. My classmates said we would empty out a couple of bottles and fill them with some choice urine. The club owner came back to the farmer's house, I suppose very angry. The farmer must have known that the time for justice had come, but he was in a bind for an answer. I didn't know how they settled it, but the club owner never went back for whiskey.

The farmer said that was a dirty trick to play on him. I said welshing on a bet was not too nice either. I told him, welshers on bets usually died right at the table. He was lucky, he was still breathing. I told the farmer there were four of us and one of him, not to bet against those odds. Whatever happened to me, would happen to him.

I told him about what I did to his friend when he asked me to steal gasoline from the farmer's auto and put it into his auto, in turn he would let me use the auto. "And I refused to steal from you," I said. "I told him to ask you for some gasoline, but he said he was embarrassed to ask because he had done so many times before."

The friend had said to me, "Just this one time," and he would never ask me again. He said he was dangerously low on fuel and probably did not have enough to get home. I decided to teach him a lesson he would never forget. I took two gallons of kerosene from the tractor fuel tank and put it into his auto.

There was enough gasoline in the auto to get the auto warm enough to run on kerosene. We started the tractor on gasoline and when the carburetor got hot, we would switch to kerosene.

About a quarter of a mile up the road, the kerosene got to the hot carburetor. The auto became a crop duster. You could not see the auto for the blue smoke. He did not dare to return to the farm, he just kept going. The police didn't catch him because most of the road to his home was through the back country.

I wonder why he never again asked me to steal?

Christmas Time in a Small Town

The year was 1917, I was three years old. The excitement was everywhere. People were caroling on the sidewalk outside our house, and everyone seemed excited about something. I did not know what was taking place, why all the hustle and bustle? I too felt festive because there were a lot of things happening. I was trying to put the activities together and trying to comprehend.

I liked the stories about a baby being born in a manger, but I didn't know what a manger was. Also, people were talking about a fellow called "Santa" who had a sleigh and eight reindeer that could fly through the air and go up and down chimneys. At that early age, I was dubious and had a problem with that one. I was not going to tell anyone about my reluctance to believe, because we were told he was a "know it all" and if we were bad boys, he would pass us by. I knew I was not always an angel, but I tried to obey and not cause too much furor most of the time.

We were told he would fill our stockings with lots of toys and candy if we were good children. We would be really good right before Christmas. Why take a risk that he would find us out for the little brats that we could sometimes be?

I remember the smell of cookies and bread baking and could hardly wait until I could get my little hand in the cookie jar, as the saying goes. My father brought a large evergreen tree into the house, put it into a pail of water and attached it to the wall so it would not fall over. I wondered what the tree was for and why he brought it in. I liked the tree because it was so green and most of the trees outside did not have any leaves on them. Only the pine and spruce trees were green. It was so cold outside and I wondered why some trees stayed green.

My older brother and sister made rings of colored paper and assembled them into chains and swags and hung them on the tree. They strung popcorn and made assimilated pearls and put them all around the tree. There were a few glass ornaments that they found and something called tinsel. It was very interesting and pretty, but what was it all about? I learned later that they were celebrating the birth of Jesus, the Savior of the world. Christmas morning came and we rushed downstairs to see what we had received. There was an orange, some sugar candy, chocolate drops and a small toy in each child's stocking. I must have been a greedy child. I was told that this Santa fellow would fill the stockings and then go up the chimney, but my stocking was far from being full. I reasoned that the measure had met my behavior, but I didn't say a word to anyone about it. Years later I got the answer. We were living in poverty, but my father did the best he could with us. We were lucky there was food in the house. We knew that food was scarce, but did not know anything about the economic conditions. We just ate and slept. That was about all we could do in a small house with so many people living there. In those days we did not have radios or television. We had one thing called a phonograph and some rollers that we would put into it, then we would turn the crank to wind it and put a needle into the reproducer—presto, music. We listened to the same music everyday. We only had a few rollers.

All the children had to attend school beginning at eight years of age and continuing through the eighth grade. High school was optional.

There was no kindergarten in those days, primarily because there were no school buses and some children had to walk as far as two miles to school through snow or rain, no matter how inclement the weather. The schoolhouse was divided into two rooms. First, second, third, and fourth grades were on one side and the four higher grades were on the other side. Each room had a big pot belly stove in the center. By the time we arrived at the school house, someone had been there and had a fire going. It felt so good to get warm after a long walk.

On my first day in school, I was a little apprehensive about what might happen. It wasn't so bad. The teacher greeted us with a big smile and said, "We will sing a few songs and then we will have prayer and a pledge allegiance to the flag of the United States of America." This broke the tension, then the teacher said she would show us how to write our names. That was challenging, but we mastered it.

I was eager to find out about everything. There was so much that we did not know. It was hard to believe we knew so little, but we had no preschooling, not even by our parents. In fact, the writing tablet and pencil were the first schooling we'd had. We could have all the paper and pencils as long as we used them properly.

I was very attentive and followed instructions. As we approached Christmas time, each of the students had to learn a stanza of the Christmas play. Then on the evening before Christmas we would recite the play in the presence of our parents. The teacher would prompt us if we became tongue-tied with stage fright. She certainly came in handy. Rehearsals were fine, but the real thing was quite different.

The plays always opened with a cute little girl bouncing out onto the stage. She would stop, swish her long hair and say, "What are you looking at me for? I haven't anything to say, so just content your eager hearts and listen to the play." Then she would retreat to the place from which she came and the play would continue.

I remember the plays as being very well done. After the ceremony there were lots of goodies for all and we would exchange little presents.

The school provided a Christmas tree for each room and we all took part in trimming it. The students were always eager to have Christmas come because it was the highlight of the year. It also helped us ignore all the cold weather. As we grew older, we appreciated the true meaning of Christmas and I learned what gold, frankincense and myrrh were. Gold, of course is a precious metal. Frankincense is an aromatic gum or resin from trees in East Africa, used as an incense and medically used as a stimulant and cough medicine. Myrrh is also a gum, a resin that exudes from trees and shrubs from Arabia and Abyssinia, and it is also used as a medicine.

One year the students from the upper grades put on a full dress presentation, complete with the baby in the manger. It certainly added a lot to our understanding of Christmas.

The church at which we attended Sunday School was about two miles from our home. We received a gold bar for each year that we had a perfect attendance. We were also given merit badges for doing extra things for the church. One year at Christmas time, when my brother and I were in our early teens, the Sunday School teacher asked for someone to volunteer to go into the woods and fetch a large evergreen tree for the church. They said it would have to be at least fourteen feet tall. My brother and I said we would go and get the tree.

We took our hatchet and went into the woods, about a mile away. It was not difficult to find a suitable tree and we chopped it down, attached a rope harness to the tree and started back to church. Most of the way was down a slight grade and through open fields. The first part of the return was easy. The snow in the woods was only a foot deep and the tree slid right along. When we reached the open field the snow was much deeper. The tree became harder and harder to pull, for it was covered with snow and it had started to rain. The snow turned to slush and froze to the tree. It was getting so heavy that at one time we thought we weren't going to be able to get the tree to the church. Also, the last part of the trip was up a steep grade. We decided to take a short route through the cemetery where the grade was not so steep. We tugged and inched our way along, finally arriving at the church.

There were some men who helped take the tree into the vestibule where the ice and snow would melt from the limbs. A lot of Sunday School boys and girls helped trim the tree. That part of town had electricity and that made it possible to attach some lights to the tree.

We learned a lot from that experience. We especially learned not to volunteer for a job that was too big for us.

I am now eighty-one years old and have seen many plays and Christmas trees. The outstanding memory that rings in my ears is that little girl's voice, "What are you looking at me for? I haven't anything to say, so just content your happy hearts and listen to the play."

Teenager's Trucking Company

My first big financial venture. The year was 1933, when I was nineteen years of age.

My name is Roger. I was born in a beautiful mountain town called Big Piney. It could have been called heaven on earth. Peace, quiet and honesty were the attributes that made living there utopia.

There was a fast flowing brook that ran through the town called Tub Mill Run. It was named after a tub mill that used the water for power. They manufactured a large assortment of wooden tubs, of which a lot were used in those days.

There was a steel mill called a foundry that melted steel and made a lot of repair parts for the railroad train that serviced the area.

There was also a large lumber company that sawed and sold lumber for local use and shipped lumber to out of town customers.

Most of the people worked at the factories and that was about all the employment available. The great economic depression had played havoc with the economy, so the factories operated on a limited basis. One had to find work anywhere he could. I was fortunate to have a part-time job working on the Mom and Pop Berger farm, which was nearby. I was paid a dollar a day and given two farmhouse meals. I averaged three days a week in the summer but less in the off season months. I had another job delivering groceries for the local store, owned by Butch and Hans. It was a strange job, called full-time, but I only worked when there were groceries to be delivered. When I was called to deliver an order, I had to do it that day or evening. I kept their old pickup truck in my possession so it was easy to get around in a hurry. They paid me nine dollars a week and that included delivering on Sunday if necessary.

I was the middle child of seven and we all did whatever we could to supplement the household income. I was very ambitious, always looking for a new way to get something extra. It was difficult, ideas came and went, little happened.

Three years passed and the Fair Labor Standards Act became law. If Butch and Hans wanted to keep me on a full-time basis, they would have to pay me the minimum wage of eighteen dollars a week. They told me to bring the truck to the store, we had to talk. Eighteen dollars a week was too much money for them to pay me for what I was doing. I played it cagey. I said, "The monkey is on your back." I knew if they let me go they would have to find someone familiar with the territory who would be willing to drive through deep snow and icy roads. They couldn't ask me to take less salary, the law was the law. Also, they needed someone reliable and willing to work those hours.

One of the advantages that went with the job was that on Saturday night after the store closed, I could take a lot of the left over ripe produce home at no cost to me, especially the over ripe bananas. I was afraid Butch and Hans would terminate my scavenging privilege, but they didn't. Everything went along as usual. Also in that year, 1936, Social Security became law. It was not much of an asset for the time being, but it was something in place of nothing. That gave me a sort of false hope for the future.

The old delivery truck was getting quite worn and I had a difficult time keeping it in repair. Just when I was really discouraged, Butch and Hans presented me with a new three-quarter-ton Plymouth van. Wow! What a thrill to drive it. The groceries would not freeze in bad weather in this van. I was one happy fellow.

I was always coming up with easier ways to do things, and I still laugh at the meat grinder I rigged up back on the farm. I scrounged up two pulleys from a friend at the

Foundry and got a pulley belt from the grain threshing machine. I attached one of the pulleys to the automobile wheel that I had put up on blocks and connected the other pulley to the meat grinder. We had several hundred pounds of meat to grind. It worked very well and I was given some smoked sausage for my ingenious device because it saved a lot of time and hard labor.

I kept dreaming of someway to do something of major importance. I kept my eyes and ears open.

Finally my big break came. One of the fellows that I had gone to school with had gotten married, and in order to have some income, he had bought a ton and a half stake rack truck and was picking up milk from farms and delivering it to the central creamery, where they made several dairy products. Billy, the owner of the truck, was as ambitious as I, and I was impressed with his accomplishment. He was a very small man, but he could pick up a ten gallon can of milk, which weighed about ninety pounds, and put it on to the truck with ease.

I decided to run along with Billy on the milk route to get out into the morning air and to have the opportunity to talk with the farmers. Talking to people was about the only way to get the news and listen to the stale jokes that you had heard a dozen times.

One day one of the farmers asked me if I knew anyone that would buy Locust Tree logs. I said, "None that I know of, but I would see what I could do to find a buyer." Hugo Snyder, the farmer, said he would pay me ten percent of the selling price of the logs if I could find a buyer. I didn't ask him for a contractual agreement because he was a big burly man. Hugo was a fitting name for him. I was meek and was not about to question his integrity. I just took his word for the agreement. After all, I didn't have the slightest idea where to look for a buyer. Hugo said he would cut the trees into logs and place them on a loading platform for a stipulated price, which at the moment escapes me.

I kept thinking, ten percent, wow, that is a lot of money. My ambition just wouldn't quit. I kept thinking, how can I find a buyer? I felt like a nut asking people to buy logs. I was dating Dorothy, my neighbor's daughter, the sweetest one and only, heaven on earth girl. Davis, her father, worked for the Twentieth Century Lumber Company. I thought of asking him if he knew of a buyer, but decided not to, lest he think I was nuts. One day I asked Dorothy to ask him. She said, "Ask him yourself, what's the matter with you? Are you embarrassed to ask him yourself?" I said, "Yes." After several days, I got up the courage and asked him. Surprise! He said, "Talk to Mr. Winthrop at the lumber company. He might help you, he is a pretty nice fellow. " It took me several days to brace myself and get the courage to talk to such an important man (little me, big man). I rehearsed my sales talk and re-rehearsed it. I practiced how I would stand, or sit if he asked me. In short, I was just plain scared to talk to a big business man.

I took the plunge and walked into his office, identified myself and asked him if he needed any locust logs. He said he had all the trees that he needed and that Locust logs were not good for sawing lumber, it was too hard to drive nails into and the wood grain was not as valuable as that of some other woods. I said, "Thank you very much." I was surprised, he shook my hand and said, "I'm John Winthrop. I will check around to see if I can help find you a buyer." I suspected he was just being nice to a young fellow. I had no faith in the meeting. One thing though, I had overcome the fear of asking big men for big favors.

That was a milestone in my life. About three days later I received a letter from the Twentieth Century Lumber Company. I hesitated to open it. In the upper left hand corner of the envelope was the name "John Winthrop, President, The Twentieth Century Lumber Company," and the address of the company. The envelope was sort of bulky for just an ordinary "thanks but no thanks" letter. I said to myself, "Open it," which I did. Much to my surprise, it contained a contract for all the Locust logs I could deliver. Eight to ten inch minimum diameter and in increments of five feet in length. The price he would pay, cash on delivery, was fair. I rushed over to the farmer, Hugo, and told him the good news. The price was acceptable to him. Hugo said, "When do you want me to start cutting?" Reality had set in. What was I doing? I had a contract to sell the logs, I had the logs available, but I did not have a truck to haul the logs. I was scared. I read the contract over carefully. It was a relief to learn that there was a conditional delivery obligation, both parties, no logs, no pay, no default liability. Dumb luck had saved me. I did not realize the trouble I could have been in.

I had three hundred and sixty-two dollars and the clothes on my back. On my combined salary of about twenty-one dollars a week, I soon found out that no truck dealer would sell me a truck of needed size and price. I kept going to every dealer, hoping against hope that one of them might sell me a truck. I felt like a kiwi bird fluttering around, unable to get off the ground. I had insufficient money for a down payment on the truck and start up expenses. I had not even thought of start up funds. My ambition to make money sort of blinded my thinking. On the other hand, if I didn't have a contract, what good would a truck be? Suddenly it came to me. "Ask Billy. Billy is smart. He knows how to get a truck, he will have the answers. Why didn't I think of Billy before?" My ambition and planning had me cornered.

Billy asked me for the contracts so he could review them. He was satisfied that a good profit could be made from the endeavor. I was right, for a change! Billy had the solution to getting a suitable truck. He suggested we form a partnership. He would put up his truck, which was paid for in full. I would put up my cash and that would give us the capitol we needed.

Again I did a stupid thing. I had only a verbal agreement

with Billy. After all, we were honest and trustworthy people, no need for formalities among friends of long standing, living only a few houses apart. WRONG. Billy suggested we buy a four ton capacity truck, that way we could make more money and the larger truck would have better tires and better brakes. We contracted for the truck and notified everyone to set the operation into motion. The truck would be delivered within a few days and we could get started. WRONG. The driver that was delivering the truck to us slid on the icy road, struck a concrete abutment and heavily damaged the front end of the truck.

The dealer said that he did not have another truck like the one we ordered in stock, but he could repair the damage within a week and it would be as good as new.

Billy, who was going to drive the truck over dangerous narrow roads with steep hills, decided we better look for another truck. I agreed and we went from dealer to dealer. There was not one truck in the area like the one we wanted. Finally, we went to see Big Ed, the Ford dealer. Big Ed was a jolly sort of guy, and easy to get along with, but he only had a five ton capacity truck in stock. The same story, if we ordered a four ton capacity we would have to wait. The original truck was $1,250.00. The Ford was $1,825.00, but it was a five ton capacity. I said to Big Ed, "Our budget will not allow for the extra cost of the truck." Big Ed said he would reduce the price in order to help us, but we would have to take the truck right away. If we went shopping elsewhere, we could forget the adjusted price. Billy and I had to make a decision. He said, "Let's flip a coin." I said this was too big of a decision to be made on a gamble. Finally, Billy asked my opinion. I said, "Let's go for it." Big Ed prepared the title and at last, we had a truck. I climbed into the truck and it was a real big vehicle. It overwhelmed me, I drove the little truck, but I was glad I did not have to drive this one. It didn't bother Billy one bit, he enjoyed the huge beast, as I named it.

Billy said, "Go ahead Roger, get behind the wheel and start it up, let's go for the maiden voyage." I said, "Nuts to you, you drive it." We went for the thrill of our lives in our new truck—well, sort of ours, we had quite a few payments and then it would be ours. Anyway, we were in business, in a big way. We delivered a load of logs and were paid in cash, just as John said. I said to Billy, "Look at this fistful of real cash. One of these days we will have a truckload of those greenbacks." (I was joking of course.)

I took out our ten percent, gave Billy his driver's pay and opened a bank account. I wrote Hugo a check for the logs and our first transaction was complete.

I said to myself, "Roger had done it. But what about the genius, Billy? Roger orchestrated the venture, but without Billy, Roger could not have consummated it. ROGER'S EGO JUST BURST. OH WELL, WE DID IT."

Billy was understanding and pleased that we were on our way to a good money making business. I had to stop thinking "I" and start thinking "WE." It looked like we were on easy street.

The logs were being used for highway guard rail posts, so there was an endless market for them. Also, there were other Locust timber woods to obtain logs from. I worked out an agreement with Billy. He would receive a driver's pay plus half the profits. I would look for new ways to make money with the truck. Billy would collect the money and deposit it into the bank account. He would keep out cash for operating expenses and pay for them on an as needed basis.

Billy went in his way and everything was running smoothly. Billy and his wife, Esther, bought new furniture for their house and a lot of toys for their baby girl. Everything was going along smoothly and it appeared we were on top of the world.

I got busy soliciting return loads in order to increase our profits. John, the lumber dealer, gave us a job hauling the sawed limber to the railroad's freight station. It was a return load and cash on delivery. The lumber was loaded onto the truck and unloaded at the freight station by huge overhead cranes. There was no physical labor involved and the pay for hauling was very good.

Just when everything appeared to be running right on schedule, TROUBLE, DOUBLE TROUBLE. One day while I was sitting in the restaurant in town having some real old fashion country cooking, Billy drove up in front of the restaurant with a load of sawed lumber. He came into the restaurant and said, "How are you doing, Roger?" I said, "Why all the formalities, how about joining me for lunch?" Billy said he didn't have time for lunch, all he wanted was five dollars for gasoline for the truck. I said, "Billy, the bank is right across the street and it is open." His faced turned pale. I asked him if he felt alright. He said, in a typical truck driver's voice, "Just give me the five dollars and let me get out of here." He said, "I'll see you this evening and explain what happened." I gave him the money and he climbed into the truck and left. I tried to imagine what had gone wrong, the truck didn't have any damage and I had not heard anything from the police.

I finished my lunch and went over to the bank to see if I could find out anything. Beady Eyes, the banker, was one of those unforgettable characters. He was tall, with white hair. He wore rimless pinched nose glasses and had a poker face. He hardly ever changed his expression, and operated like a robot, you never knew what he was thinking.

For starters, I decided to ask him how much money was in our checking account. He walked over to the cash drawer, took out a silver half dollar and bounced it onto the marble top Teller's counter. I said, "Sir, I don't believe you understood me. I would like to know how much money is in our account." Beady eyes went to a file drawer and handed me our account papers. He opened them to the last page, looked at me and said, "Fifty cents."

I noticed most of the checks had been made out to his father-in-law, Walter, and his brother-in-law, Peter. I was puzzled as to why Billy would lend those two dead beats money, especially almost eight hundred dollars.

About six o'clock in the evening, Billy drove up in front of my house, got down on his knees and started crying. Sort of under his breath he said, "Roger, forgive me. It will never happen again." I said, "WHAT HAVE YOU DONE?" He stood up, braced himself, and said he had gotten into a poker game with his in-laws and had lost all our money. He said he would make it up to me and begged forgiveness. I said, "Those worthless so and so's never did an honest day's work in their lives." Billy said, "Don't criticize them, they won it fair and square." I said, "Billy, those two never did anything on the level. They are card sharks." Billy asked me what I was going to do about the situation. I said, "I'm trapped, I have no choice in the matter. Get into the truck and get out of here." He handed me the money for the day's transaction, but I told him to keep it, he would need it to keep the truck on the road. He thanked me for being so understanding and drove away. I did not understand my feelings at the time, I was calm and didn't get upset. Somehow I felt time would heal the wound, or the wound would wound the heal, as the saying goes. For a while I kept a close check on the entire business operation and everything went along as Billy promised. I decided he had learned a lesson and the money we had lost was an expensive asset to future business dealings in our partnership.

WRONG AGAIN!

One evening Big Ed, the Ford dealer, drove up in front of the house in a classy convertible with wire spoke wheels, a rumble seat and lots of shiny trim.

I said, "Bid Ed, you are a real salesman, but I cannot afford the classy chassis." Big Ed thanked me for the compliment, but said he was not there to sell me an auto. He said, " Your partner has run out of acceptable promises or should I say bare faced lies." I asked how much was in default. Big Ed said, "A lot, three months of installments."

He said he was sorry to inform me that the Sheriff would be along in a few minutes, just in case I offered lies instead of cash. Big Ed said, "You must know what is going on in your business and you didn't call me." I suppose I acted in haste at the thought of losing the truck, which meant I would lose my contracts also. I went into the house and took almost every penny I had and handed it to Big Ed. He apologized for being so presumptuous, handed me a receipt for the money, told the Sheriff he had been satisfied and went down the road.

Billy passed the Sheriff on the way home and was curious to know what had transpired. He came over to my house and asked what the Sheriff wanted. I said, "That is an easy question to answer, three months overdue payments or the truck." Again Billy went into his crying act. He promised God and man that it would never happen again. He also thanked me for not telling his very honest father and mother about his wrong doings.

I said, "Billy, you are sick, get help. I cannot help you." I was more dumbfounded than angry. I realized that I had a big problem. I could not drive the truck and keep my other two jobs. Also I was afraid to drive that big monster of a vehicle, especially loaded with those heavy logs. I needed time to think. I turned my back on Billy and didn't say another word. Billy got into the truck and drove off. I again would have to wait and see what happened.

I will never understand why I thought Billy would reform. Occasionally, I would check on the bank account and all was in order. Again he was able to deceive me.

Three months later, Big Ed arrived. He just smiled and held out his hand. I said, "Wait here." I went into the house and got my set of keys to the truck. I said, "Just go over there and release the boom chains and take the jacks out from under the springs, let the logs roll off onto the earth, the truck is yours.

Billy heard the commotion and came running to see what was happening. I said, "Billy, in a manner of speaking, you just went over the cliff to destruction. In fact, you hit rock bottom, you have had it, get lost." He said, "Please do something to save us," and started his begging for another chance act. I said, "You betrayed a trust that you swore to God. Who could trust you?" Esther, his wife, asked me to reconsider. They were losing the truck and their livelihood. When I told her and his father and mother the whole story, it was difficult for them to comprehend how he could be so dishonest and inconsiderate.

Billy got a job in a clay mine where it was always very damp. He contracted pneumonia a few years later and died. Esther got a job in the grocery store and supported herself and their daughter.

I went to New York and used my experience to become a good business man. I had learned a hard lesson, but never became bitter about the matter. I realized that I was a little man in a big man's world. I had learned one thing. If you have a partner, have a good business attorney.

Country Boy
Automobile
Chauffeur

The year was 1930. I was an ambitious fellow named Roger living in a small mountain town, always looking for some way to earn some extra money.

I was sixteen years old on my most recent, long awaited birthday. At last, I could get a learner's automobile driving permit. I memorized all of the rules and regulations. I wanted to be sure I passed the state test to get my driver's license.

Actually, driving the automobile was easy. I had a lot of practice driving around the farm fields. Once in while, I would take the automobile out onto the country road late at night. The automobile was a 1917 R.E.O. touring car, very big and very difficult to drive.

The big day came on which I was scheduled to take the test. A neighbor came to the rescue. He had just purchased a Chrysler four door. He let me drive it to town, thirty miles away, where they made you pass a written test, drive the automobile as directed by a state policeman, and answer some questions about the rules of the road. I was never that close to a policeman before, and I was a little apprehensive, but I kept my mind on what I was supposed to do.

The policeman sat with me for a few minutes, signed some papers and said, "Take these inside and give them to the desk clerk," (who was also a policeman). "Have a seat over there with those other people." Neither of the officers gave me any indication whether I had passed or flunked the test. After a few minutes, the desk clerk called me to the desk and said, "Congratulations, you are now licensed to drive an automobile, until it becomes necessary for us to revoke it for violating the law, should that ever become necessary. Drive safely and obey the law. We are here to protect you. Good-bye and good luck."

I virtually ran out of the automobile to tell my neighbor that I had gotten my license. I thanked him for accompanying me to the testing station and letting me drive his automobile. I said that if there was anything I could do for him, to just let me know. He said his wife did not know how to drive and he would appreciate it if I took her to wherever she wanted to go.

My neighbor's name was John, his wife's name was Alice, and they had a fourteen-year-old daughter named Fern. It was obvious why Fern's parents were nice to me, for they made sure their little darling was near when I was present. They asked me to teach Fern to drive, which was not easy. In those days, there was no power assisted steering and no automatic gear shifting. If you had to make a difficult turn, you had to use brute force. Fern weighed about ninety pounds (soaking wet), and was definitely not a brute. She had difficulty steering the vehicle.

Another challenge was shifting gears. When you wanted to start the vehicle, you had to set the parking brake, put the gearshift into neutral then put your left foot onto the starter button and press it. When the engine started, you would have to press the clutch pedal to the floor and put the gearshift lever into the low gear position. Then, you would release the clutch and apply pressure to the gasoline accelerator pedal. When the automobile reached a speed of about ten miles per hour, you had to depress the clutch pedal, put the gearshift lever into the second gear position and release the clutch pedal. At twenty miles per hour, you had to press the clutch pedal, put the shift lever into the high gear position and release the clutch. Then you would accelerate as necessary to maintain the speed you desired. This procedure was necessary every time you stopped and wanted to start again. When you stopped, you had to press the clutch pedal to the floor and put the gearshift into neutral, then release the clutch. To go into reverse, you had to press the clutch to the floor and put the shift lever into the reverse position and release the clutch. All this shifting was as boring as it is to read about. Just think of how the automatic transmission does about ninety percent of the shifting, knowing just when to do everything for you. With either type of transmission, you can shift into a low gear to help keep the automobile from going too fast downhill. It also assists the braking.

The Chrysler automobile was equipped with hydraulic brakes for the first time around 1928, which made it so much easier to stop the vehicle. Most motor vehicles have hydraulic brakes, especially trucks and buses.

John and Alice took a liking to most of the teenagers in the neighborhood and they had one of the few radios in town. They would let us listen to *Amos and Andy* and *The News by Lowell Thomas*, then they would tell us to scoot.

The radio was a cathedral style, battery operated Philco. It was what they called in those days a loud speaker. Most radios had headphones. Radio batteries were expensive and were not long lasting like the batteries that are available today. You needed three batteries, an "A" battery, a "B" battery and a "C" Battery (radios were not yet invented to operate on house electricity).

John liked me because he could trust me with his new automobile, which he let me borrow on several occasions. He would do anything to keep me near to his beautiful daughter. Alice too was pleased when her darling was near when I was present.

It didn't work out too well with Fern and I. I had a girlfriend that kept my attention, she was sixteen and in high school, her name was Mable. Fern was fourteen and in the seventh grade. The teenagers would have called me a cradle robber if I had dated her. Mable was a beautiful redhead, with a shape that diverted my thoughts from other girls, she also had a way of convincing me that she was mine.

One day Fern came into the farm field to pick daisies and strawberries and I was picking daisies and strawberries. In retrospect, I think I must have been dumb, but I really didn't want to encourage her to do something that we shouldn't. She looked like she was disappointed, but she understood. I was cruising in neutral, but it was not easy, I just did not want to get involved with her. I believe that she just wanted to be friendly, but I used to think that every girl that looked at me was interested in doing what came naturally. What an ego I had.

I was inexperienced, except for what the red head was teaching me. She was a good teacher, and I was an eager student. She had a hold on me and was not letting go. We were very careful not to get into any trouble, her father would have killed both of us.

Mable knew I was very loyal, and I would not betray her trust. She had her own version of "you will never get to heaven if you break the rules between us." Mable's sister, Dorothy, knew what Mable and I were doing, but she would not tell on us. She was a very loyal friend. I knew she would have liked to experiment, but was not going to share her sister's pleasures with me.

I actually thought enough of Dorothy that if I hadn't been involved with her sister, she would have been a good person for me to marry. I thought that much of her. Time and tide let all three of us drift apart. I believe that is the destiny of a lot of teenagers.

My first big chauffeuring job came when Sophie, a widow lady, bought a big Pontiac touring automobile. She was very rich, her husband had been a shipper of trainloads of coal to Baltimore and Washington, D.C. Sophie inherited the business, and a lot of money. Delmar, her husband, died in a very strange accident. He was shoveling the snow in front of their house when a big icicle fell onto his head. He died before anyone knew the accident had happened. The icicle was several feet long and weighed quite a few pounds. It fell from the roof, which was about fifteen feet high.

Sophie had a lot of business transactions to take care of and the courthouse and legal businesses were thirty miles away. I took her on a lot of chauffeuring trips and she paid me two dollars a day. If we were on the road at mealtime, she would even pay for my food. Sophie lavished me with gifts at holiday time, buying me a chauffeur's cap, jacket, tie and driver's gloves. I expressed much appreciation for the items, but felt like a nut wearing them. I suppose it eased part of her ego, although she didn't put on too much ritz. She was old-fashioned.

At the end of the trip and close to dinner time, she would invite me to join them in a delicious meal and have a piece of homemade mince meat pie that was better than the best. She sure knew how to cook.

We had no personal interest in one another. I was a kid and she was an old lady, possibly fifty. Alas, she had a twenty-three-year-old daughter and the daughter's two children living with her, a boy and girl about four years old. Janice, the daughter, was married but she had a worthless husband that would not get a job. He would walk into the house, stay a few weeks, and just walk away for months at a time. It didn't occur to me to ask if he contributed to the support of the family; it was none of my concern.

Mama had lots of gold, and didn't mind spending it. She was not a spend thrift, but she was very generous. Helping others made her happy. I suppose it was her way of thanking God that she was so fortunate, because most of the people in the town were not very well blessed.

Sophie made it very easy for me to be alone with Janice, her dear little darling that could do no wrong. After dinner, Sophie would take a walk over to her sister Molly's house, which was about a quarter of a mile away. She had the choice of walking the country road, or the railroad track. Either way, we could see her coming and going. As soon as her mother left, Janice would put the children to bed, have a shower, and slip into a house coat. Today, we call it "getting into something comfortable." Janice would then stretch out on the sofa.

We both knew that Mama would allow us at least two hours. It was up to me to decide what I was going to do. I had made up my mind that I would not fall into the trap, at least not go too far with the game. Of course, I was not the angel that I professed to be in the beginning of this story. I too had to do something to pass the time (poor excuse), so I would stretch out on the sofa beside her. We would hold hands and take deep breathing exercises. Cuddling and kissing took up most of the time. I kept telling myself that anything else was a NO. At a time like that, "no" is almost possible.

In this case, it was impossible. Sometimes I wished Mama would come home quickly. Anyway, I escaped unscathed. I like to think I was the first flat tire on Sophie's trip to encourage me to make Janice happy.

One day, Sophie asked Janice how we were making out. Janice said, "He is as harmless as a dove." It was a wonder that I didn't cross the line, Janice was as pretty as a picture, with long blond hair, a great smile and a shape that made you take a second look. Oh alright, three looks. I suppose Mama wondered what was wrong with me. I was afraid she would stop being so generous to me, but she continued her monetary blessings.

One evening, Janice and I went to the river to cut ice for the ice cream freezer. In those days, we made our own ice cream, the ingredients were blended and cooked, then we would put the mixture in the center container and put ice all around the can that contained the cooked mixture. Next we would put salt over the ice to make it melt. We turned the handle to rotate the can and mixing paddles. After about fifteen minutes, or when our arms were very tired we would have delicious ice cream.

Pardon me for digressing from the trip to the river. When we were out of site, Janice opened her robe and said, "This is how cold you are to me. You know I need you. When are you going to do something about it?" I said leaving her alone was very difficult for me too. "Think of your children and worthless husband. I wish you were not obligated, I would be pleased to warm you."

Sophie's bother-in-law, Big John, had a scrap metal and animal fur trading business. Big John would buy metal and when he had a railroad car full, he would ship it to Pittsburgh, Pennsylvania to the steel smelting foundry. He also bought scrap rubber for recycling. He made a good living from his enterprises and he lived in a colonial style house. He kept the scrap metal and rubber in a big barn located across the road from his residence. John was quite a character, he was seven feet tall and weighed about two-hundred and fifty pounds. He was a big, burly fellow, with a wrinkled face bearing the complexion of an outdoorsman. As I would define him, he was rough and ready. He was a very nice person and I am confident that he never cheated anyone. He would offer you a fair price and say, "Su Bud, take it or leave it." He used the saying "Su Bud" as a by word. I never found out what it meant and I wonder if Big John even knew.

I agreed to use my old automobile and charge him four dollars, which was twice as much as chauffeuring him in his vehicle would cost. He advised me that the trip would be about fifty miles of rough going, because the roads were rough and muddy and we would encounter snow and ice. I said, "In that case, I would like to have fifty cents more for the gasoline." He said, "No problem," and we agreed. Gasoline was seventeen cents a gallon in those days. I was soon to learn that I was going on a trip that would be beyond my wildest imagination.

The temperature was forty degrees Fahrenheit, just the

right temperature for melting snow and ice and turning the road into a sea of mud. The first two miles were on an improved road; it was easy going. Then Big John said, "Turn right at the next farm road and go up to the farm house." I had to put the tire chains on to keep going.

The fur trappers knew when Big John would be at their places to buy furs, and they usually greeted Big John with broad smiles. Big John never smiled, he would just say, "Su Bud young fellow, how are things with you? Hope you had a good catch." The fur trapper would present his pelts one at a time. Big John was a bargainer. He usually said, "Nice large pelt, but caught out of season, you should wait for very cold weather before trapping the animals. The fur is much thicker and shinier, more valuable." Big John would then say, "Su Bud," and offer a low price. They would bargain and finally Big John would make his last offer. The trapper would agree most of the time. This dickering would go on one fur at a time. Big John would pull out his big bag full of silver coins and pay the trapper. Everyone got paid in silver, Big John said it gave them a sense of getting more, if they did not get paper money. He was a shrewd buyer.

Along about noon time, Big John said, "There is a small country store about a half mile up the road, stop there." He pulled out his dollar Ingersol watch and said it was lunch time. I didn't have anything with me for lunch and also didn't have any money. Big John went into the store and I followed him, just in case he would offer me something. It paid off, he said to the store keeper, "Cut me a chunk of that store cheese," as it was known in the back woods. (It was mild cheddar.) He also said, "Cut me a pound of bologna." He told me to get a box of soda crackers and he paid the grocer from his coin bag. He invited me to sit on the bench by the pot belly stove. He took a big switch blade knife out of his pocket and wiped the blade off on his dirty pants leg.

I was surprised by his action, but I was hungry and this was not the time to worry about cleanliness. He cut us each a chunk of cheese and bologna. With one flip of the knife, the cracker box was open. What a picture we must have made sitting there eating. I didn't see anything to drink, so I ignored my thirst. We finished lunch and Big John said "Su Bud, it's time to get on the road." I think that was about the one hundredth time I had heard that idiotic term "Su Bud." In fact, I was looking forward to getting home so I wouldn't have to hear it again. I believe he was not aware of what he was saying. Big John just kept going forward, never recanting. It was a style that was making money for him. You never knew whether to like him or be annoyed at him.

What turned out to be a very exhausting day finally came to an end. The automobile was covered with mud and the gasoline tank was almost empty. Big John took out his money bag and handed me four silver dollars and a silver half dollar. My disappointment must have shown because he looked me straight in the eye and said, "You should have asked for more." He did not offer me more. I believe he was trying to teach me a lesson, not to bargain when you have no idea of what you were getting into. We remained good friends, and I drove his rattle trap around town for him at a price of two dollars a day. Only once was I invited to dinner at his house. It was Thanksgiving Day and he had all the in-laws and out-laws over for a feast. I was the out-law, not being a relative.

There were two strange chauffeuring jobs that I encountered. One of them involved a young man from out of town whose automobile I would drive sixty-five miles to a red light district, always on a Wednesday night. He liked girls of different types and colors. He had a new car and dressed very well. He was well educated, but he liked variety. The round trip took five hours and he paid me a dollar per hour. He preferred to pay by the hour because he would sometimes stay longer or stop on the way home for beer.

He often invited me to join his parties in the red-light district, but I declined his offers. I would take his automobile and go down to a safe part of town and park near the theater where there were lots of people around. At ten thirty, I would drive to the alley and if he was not there, I would drive past the alley every half hour until he was ready to head for home. We never discussed what he did or why he went there.

The other strange case was a single man, Albert. He was a World War I veteran, had a purple heart and walked with a limp. I asked him once what had happened and he said he did not want to talk about it. In fact, he didn't talk much about anything. Albert had a smooth running automobile called an "Oakland." Every Saturday night I would drive him to a small railroad town that had no stores or places of business that stayed open in the evenings. It was like a ghost town. On the way there, he would scold me for accelerating on the up grade of the little rolling hills. He said to accelerate on the grade going down hill and coast up hill. It was his automobile, and I humored him, though I could not see the logic.

I would take Albert to the railroad station, which was closed most of the time, he would get out of the automobile and just seem to disappear. I would go down the road about half a mile and park at a roadside tavern. It was safe there. At eleven o'clock, right on time, Albert would appear. I would drive him back home, collect my money and walk home. The only possibility is that he might have had a key to the railroad station and was meeting someone there. There were no lights on, in or out of the building. It was in total darkness except on moon lit nights. Even then, he would do the disappearing act.

A middle-aged man named Harry Hardwick, his wife Ester and their son Gordon, who was about twenty-five years of age, moved into our little town. They appeared to be very wealthy. They had two new automobiles and a stretch limousine. Everyone in town wondered why rich people would come to reside in a small poor town. The nosey neighbors soon found out what they were doing. (I was one of the nosey neighbors).

Harry had been sent there by a ship company to have some special steel castings made at the steel foundry. The steel foundry melted the steel in a furnace and poured it into the ship company's molds. Harry would inspect the castings to ensure they were made properly. The ship company required quite a number of castings, so it would take almost a year to complete the manufacturing of the parts.

Gordon was very mischievous, to the point of being annoying. He liked playing jokes on the teenagers, to the extent that he was obnoxious. Very few people liked him, although he was always trying to impress the girls.

If he saw a pretty girl driving her automobile, he would bump into her fender or bumper to get her attention and in hopes of getting acquainted with her. Another way he would manage to meet girls was to make blind dates with fellows and go for a limousine ride. He would hire me to drive the limousine, so he would be free to do whatever he could get away with. Gordon paid me two dollars per hour and told me his generosity was part hush money. I was to hear no evil, see no evil, or discuss any evil about what he or anyone did. As I put it to him, for two dollars per hour I could be deaf, dumb, and blind.

These trips turned out to be real eye openers. Gordon and his friends (as he referred to them) would get into the limousine and tell me to drive around, throughout the country as much as possible. Usually Gordon was the only one in the group who knew me; I would put on my chauffeur's garb and look straight ahead. Occasionally, I recognized some of them and they knew me. It didn't matter, they were having fun and were assured that I wouldn't tell, no matter what took place. I was interested in only one thing, money. Most of the girls didn't need to be impressed by education. From their actions, I knew they were not on their first trip.

Surprise! One evening my Sunday School teacher got into the limousine with his wife's sister. My face turned red and I think he turned green. I just said, "Hello, don't mind me, I only work here, I do not pay attention to other people's business, or mention it to anyone. Gordon knows I do not talk out of place, I keep my mouth shut. I am only interested in keeping this limousine going where it is supposed to go." I believe it was shock and fear that made my teacher say to me, "Quiet people graduate." I said, "I hear you."

The rest of the evening was spent having a good time. To me, it was revolting to think a person would date his wife's sister. Suppose he got her pregnant. What a mess that would make, especially in a small town. His wife was my English teacher; she was so pleasant. I felt sorry for her. None of the cheating was necessary, except for two greedy adulterers.

In class the next day, my chemistry teacher casually opened a bottle and said, "I wonder if this is still good." I sniffed it and it nearly smothered me, it was liquid, full-strength chlorine. He looked right at me and said, "See how easy it is to get hurt." It was obvious he was threatening me in a subtle way. All seemed to be shelved, nothing was ever said, and it was a forgotten issue . . . thank God.

The most disgusting chauffeuring trip I ever made was on the Fourth of July. A very rich farmer had an antiquated limousine, the model that had a glass divider between the back seats and the chauffeur. He asked me to drive him and one of his business associates around with some very young girls. The girls were probably not older than fifteen, and the farmer and his friends were over forty.

The farmer was married to a woman who was not too difficult to dislike. She thought she was God's gift to the world. Frankly, my opinion of her was that she was a gift to the five and ten, for five. However, I could not see that as being justification for her husband committing statutory rape and adultery. I didn't let it bother me. I got paid twenty dollars to drive and keep my mouth shut. However, as I look back on the incidence, there was the possibility of my being arrested for being a party to the altercation.

The farmer handed me a twenty dollar bill and told me to get the limousine, pick up the girls in back of the high school building, and get out of town. He then directed me to drive to a secluded place on top of a mountain. The girls wore scanty blouses and short shorts. They were ready to have fun. They seemed innocent, but eager. When we reached the parking place, they all got out of the limousine, took blankets and went into the woods. After about an hour, they came back to the limousine. I drove them back to the place where I picked them up.

The next day, I asked the farmer if he knew the penalty for statutory rape. He smiled and said, "They can't prove anything. In fact, if you tell on us, we will pin the offense on you. There were two of us and the girls got well paid. They would lie for us, and there's no telling what we would do to you, better keep your mouth shut."

One evening, the farmer's niece from out-of-state came to spend a few days at the farm. Her name was Diana, she was sixteen and as pretty as a picture, as they say. Diana was well endowed and had a shape that could get her anything she wanted, and she wanted. Her girlfriend introduced me to her when I picked her up at the railroad station with the limousine. The farmer wanted me to pick her up with the limousine because he wanted to impress her with what he had, and believe me, before the evening was over, she was convinced he had plenty.

Diana invited me to go with her to the swimming hole in the river past the farm field. When we got there, she took off all her clothes and said, "Come on, what are you waiting for? I am waiting for you." I decided to swim and ignore her, she was moving too fast for me. When we returned to the farmhouse, the farmer asked me if his niece was any good, I told him I chickened out. He handed me the usual twenty dollar bill and said, "Get the limousine and get her into it." I obeyed him and the two of them spent an hour and a half doing what comes naturally.

Cutie became pregnant, or possibly was pregnant. She told her mother and father that her uncle, the farmer, was the one who was going to be big daddy. Mama and Papa, Diana's parents, had the farmer arrested for statutory rape and for getting her pregnant. I was surprised that the farmer didn't try to blame it on me. The farmer offered the three of them cash to withdraw the charges and take care of the problem. The father and mother refused the offer and took the farmer to court.

I was subpoenaed as a witness. I was really scared because I could have been convicted of being an accessory to the crime by virtue of driving the limousine for illicit sex purposes.

The defense advised me to admit driving the vehicle for pay, but disclaim any knowledge of what had happened. If I was asked any more questions, I should plead the fifth. On the day of the trial, we were all sworn to tell the truth under the penalty of perjury. By now, I was sweating gum drops. The judge listened intently to the farmer's story of how he was carried away from reality by the girl's advances. The defense attorney testified about his findings about Miss Eveready's reputation in her home town. She was eveready, frequently.

The judge called all of us into his chambers and said he had reached a decision. He told the mother and father of Diana to take their pig and go home. He said that there was insufficient reason to send the farmer to prison for twenty years for this offense. Statutory rape under the statutes carried a penalty of not less than twenty years. The judge said that it wouldn't be good for any of us to be back in his courtroom. "Get out of here before I change my mind and have you all locked up. You are all guilty as hell, everyone of you contributed to this unfortunate incident." I believe I was the first one out of that courthouse.

The last limousine trip was the one that made me quit being a chauffeur. An acquaintance of mine asked me to drive his new touring automobile one Saturday evening. I asked where he wanted me to go. He said, "Just drive anywhere away from our home town."

He had arranged blind dates for a foursome. He too paid me well and I was pleased to accept the job. We picked up two beautiful young ladies at the roadside dance hall. Then I picked up his friend at the railroad station. His friend was my Sunday School teacher, a married man. We rode around for a couple of hours, and no one spoke very much. There was some hugging and kissing, but all was low key. The girls did not know what the problem was, and I suppose they were wondering why they were not being treated as well as they had expected.

I was glad when the evening was over, the shock was too much for me, it seemed like a nightmare, surely this was not happening, after all, a man stands before God and man and professes his integrity. How could he do this to his wife? I tried to convince myself that this happened in a moment of weakness. Not so, I later found out that he had a history of cheating on his wife.

I assured him that I would never divulge anything. All a good chauffeur ever sees is the road, and all he hears is the road noise. He resigned from the church and moved out of town. This convinced me that you cannot do wrong and be right. I was grateful for having the chauffeuring experience. I moved to New York City and accepted a job in a retail store . . . Chauffeuring was not for me.

Neophyte
Aircraft Pilots

The year was 1927. I was thirteen years old.

The town in which I lived was on a mountain top, 2,113 feet above sea level. It was a beautiful place to live, but there were very few employment opportunities.

The coal mines had been worked out and there were no factories. The only jobs were part-time farm work. We foraged for food from the mountains. There were plenty of berries and mushrooms. We did game hunting for food also. One of the assets of the area was a cold water spring. Nearly every morning, the fog would shroud the area. We were actually up in the clouds until around ten o'clock in the morning. When the sun would dissipate the fog, we could see three states from the fire tower on top of the mountain.

One foggy summer evening, a small airplane appeared and the pilot was looking for the emergency landing strip that was listed on his air map.

He made an approach and saw some cattle on the runway. He aborted the attempt to land and did a go around. The farmer got a white bed sheet and ran in the direction in which the pilot was to land.

The pilot thought he was signaling him not to land, so he made a big circle around the landing strip and tried to figure out what the farmer was trying to convey to him. All the helpful farmer did was confuse the issue. The pilot did another go around, and he had no choice but to land. He was running low on fuel and the nearest airport was forty miles away.

The pilot held enough altitude on landing to clear the cattle. He touched down, but could not stop before he hit the wood rail fence. The plane nosed over in the mud. The pilot was only shaken up, but the plane needed a new propeller and a few struts to replace the ones that had been bent.

Of course, almost everyone for miles around came to see the airplane wreck. It was very exciting because about the only thing that happened in that town was "the Sun came up and the Sun went down."

The farmer let the pilot sleep at his farmhouse and let him use the telephone to order parts to repair the plane. The next day a small airplane landed with the repair parts without incident. A lot of the boys from our town helped to straighten out the damaged parts and install the new ones. It was very interesting work because about the only repair we had ever done was repairing a farm plow. When we had everything in order, the pilot did a run up, as they call it, to be sure everything was working well. He taxied down to the end of the strip, applied full power and went roaring off into the blue yonder. As he came over us, he rocked the wings to let us know everything was okay.

This wet our appetites to find out more about aviation. We got all the books we could find and read them through and through several times. We were eager to learn to fly. Being eager was well and good, but without an airplane, we were not going very far. The nearest airport was forty miles away, but we would hitchhike to the airport and talk to pilots and look at airplanes. Once in a while, one of the pilots would let us go along for a ride. Some of those old crates, as we called them, were very fragile, but we were too interested in flying to be scared. Well, we were a little scared.

About a year later, we received a real thrill. Three army planes, big ones, became fogged in and had to use the emergency landing strip. One used the strip and the other two took a chance and landed in the field beside the airstrip. They landed without incident, but a problem developed. The land in the field next to the strip was too soft to allow the airplane to take off. Fortunately, it was late autumn and the earth would soon freeze. The men had to stay several weeks before they could fly out. The worst thing that happened to them was that several annoying boys kept asking questions about the airplanes.

I suppose they got tired of answering questions, but they were tolerant of us. Actually, we became good friends. We knew where to get bootleg whiskey and girls. One of the pilots gave us an airmap and a landing plate. A landing plate shows the details of one landing field.

Finally, the sad day came. Early one morning the earth was frozen. The pilots tested the hardness by driving their airplanes a short distance, it was frozen enough and they taxied to the end of their field, turned around and then with full throttle, came roaring up the field.

They barely cleared the fence, but they were airborne. The big thrill for us was, after they gained a few thousand feet, they came roaring right down over us, giving us a good-bye salute. What a treat for a couple of farm boys.

One day, the milk truck driver told us of a small airplane that had crashed, about a hundred miles away. He said it belonged to a farm boy. He was only shaken up in the crash, but the plane was heavily damaged. The boy's father would not let him fix it up or allow him to fly it. We took an old Whippet Convertible automobile and went to see if we could buy the wreck and put it back together. We were able to buy it real cheap and we tied the pieces onto and into the auto. It looked like an erector set with a motor hanging out of the trunk. If anyone had accused us of being nuts, we would not have argued with him. We were determined to repair it and fly.

We got it back to the farm and put the plane's parts onto the barn floor. Money was scarce so we decided to straighten the struts and frame. That worked out well, the propeller was bent beyond repair, so we had to save our pennies and buy a new one. The wings and rudder were made of a wood frame covered with canvas, then covered with a substance called "dope." The dope would shrink the canvas and make it like metal, but it was much lighter than metal. We were fortunate to have a good automobile mechanic to help us with the motor. It needed a bit of cleaning and adjusting, but it was a reliable motor.

The time came when we had the plane all together. Someone had to take it up on its first flight. No one wanted to be the first to test it. Also, not one of us had ever flown an airplane. We did not know what to expect once we were airborne.

We knew it would drift from side to side and feel like floating, which we would be. We decided to put an advertisement into the newspaper and sell it. I believe it was the best decision we could have agreed on. A pilot came and looked at the plane, taxied it around the farm field and decided to buy it. He said, "I will give you a thousand dollars cash as is." We were surprised! We farm boys didn't think that there was that much money on earth. We would have had to work years to earn that much money. We took the money and divided it equally between us.

The pilot took off in the plane. It flew like a bird. He was pleased and we were astonished, to say the least. We kept on visiting the airport and learning all we could about flying, I was surprised to learn that lift occurred on the top of the wing and not on the impinging airflow under the bottom of the wing. This can be confirmed by reading *Bernoulli's Principal of Airflow*.

I now had money to pay for some airplane rides and I spent my spare time talking to pilots and flying with them. One of the pilots had an open cockpit airplane, a three passenger. It had a big radial engine with no muffler. It really made a lot of noise and had a lot of horsepower. One day the owner said he was going to let me pilot it with him sitting near by. I was thrilled for a moment, then reality set in. What would I do once the wheels were off the ground and I was airborne? I said to myself that if I was ever going to fly, there would be a first time, and this was it.

I set the trim tabs, checked the magnetos, checked the carburetor heat control, and taxied to the runway. This was it. I pushed the throttle to the full power position, and the plane quickly reached flying speed. I did what pilots call "rotating," meaning that I eased back on the controls to set the altitude of attack to take off position. Suddenly, I felt the airplane leave the earth and continue in a steady climb. The fear that almost kept me on the ground diminished. I would almost say disappeared, but that was not so. I had to get back to Terra Firma.

At about a thousand feet, I banked around to the left and circled until I was lined up with the runway. I adjusted the propeller revolutions to 1,750 per minute and the plane began to lose altitude. I pulled on the carburetor heat control and lowered the flaps. I was surprised to feel the nose rise when I lowered the flaps. I pushed forward on the yoke and the plane was now on a perfect gliding decent and the earth was coming up to meet me. I just maintained my glide and the runway was only a few feet from the plane. I was at the correct airspeed of seventy miles per hour. The plane was falling just a little too quickly. I did not have time to lift the flaps, so I applied a little forward throttle to make it fly faster. They call it "dragging it in" today. I touched down with only a slight bounce and feathered the prop to 900 rpm. Then I taxied back to the hanger.

The owner complimented me on being able to control the plane. That was fine. There was no severe wind or ice to deal with. There was a lot more for me to learn.

After a few more supervised flights (the owner said anytime I wanted to fly the plane, it was okay with him), my only restrictions were that I keep in sight of the airport and not take any passengers with me.

If I ran out of money to buy gasoline for the plane, I would pick up soda bottles that had a deposit on them and scavenge for junk that I could sell to the junk dealer for cash. Gasoline was seventeen cents a gallon and one gallon would last about ten minutes once you were airborne. I needed about two gallons to be on the safe side. Flying was an expensive hobby for a boy without a job, but I was determined to become a good pilot.

I had a lot of good times flying the "Old Crate," as I called it. I later taught my buddies how to fly. Not one of us ever had a close call because we followed the survival rules.

Many years later, I formed a flying club and bought two airplanes. A four seater Cessna Skyhawk and a One Fifty Cessna Commuter with two seats. The Skyhawk had what they call a "full panel of navigation equipment," which permitted us to fly day or night. In fact, it is easier to fly at night than in the day. You can more easily see the airport control tower beacons and the lighted runways.

I taught flying for four years and the one thing I impressed on the students was that it takes sixty hours of air time before you can fly solo. It took me about an hour to teach them everything about the airplane controls, so I would use the remainder of the time to teach them how to keep from getting killed. You do not get a second chance to do the right thing. You do it while you are alive. A preflight checkup of the plane is a must.

One day I took off with the airspeed indicator not indicating the speed. I was a wise guy and sure it would function when I reached full throttle speed. I thought it was stuck. Not so, there was a bug in the Pitot tube, which supplies the information to the airspeed indicator. I was fortunate, I radioed the control tower to ask them if I could make an emergency landing and if they would hold all other planes from the runway. They approved it and I landed safely. In the air, there is nothing by which to judge airspeed because there is nothing but air to pass.

There are several things that are a must before you attempt to fly. Shake the tail end of the plane in order to wash the condensation off the underside of the wing gas tank. Wait ten minutes, then drain the fuel sump to get all the water out of the tanks. If you fail to do this, on take off, when you raise the nose of the plane, the gas will wash the condensed water off the top of the tank and into the carburetor. When you are about five hundred feet off the earth, the engine will stop and you will crash. If you fail to apply carburetor heat when the prop speed is lower than 1,750 revolutions per minute, ice will form in the carburetor. Yes, this is true even when the outside temperature is ninety degrees.

Rhyme ice will form on the leading edge of the wing if the temperature is below freezing and the air is moist. Rhyme ice will build up in seconds and looks like an ocean wave. Then it sets up a burble on top of the wing and the wing has no lift. Down you go, like a rock. The defense against this condition is to dive the minute you see ice crystals on the leading edge of the wing. Surface ice is just extra weight. It of course, effects the speed and lift of the airplane, but if you have enough power, you can fly.

The best safety device is the pilot's eye. Look ahead and look before you turn. Some other pilots may not be looking. DON'T TAKE CHANCES.

Our First House

1948 . . . East Orange New Jersey

We were living in a two room apartment, which had an efficiency kitchen closed off from the living room with two louvered doors, a small pantry, and no clothes closet. It was on the fourth floor of a very nice apartment house. It was all brick and had marble floors in the foyer and hall ways. There was a passenger elevator that ran all the way from the basement to the penthouse on the tenth floor. As there was no central air conditioning in those days, a few people had window air conditioners, but they were very expensive to purchase and operate. We would go up onto the rooftop lounge and get a breath of cool air in the evening. It made life tolerable.

We were lucky to have a small screen television. I was in the electronics business, part time. One day a lady gave me the television for installing a big aluminum antenna on the roof of the apartment house. She had just bought a twelve inch black and white television set. Color sets had not been invented by that time. One of the large manufacturers was experimenting with recording programs on magnetic tape, another one was trying to produce a color television.

The apartment was quite cozy and was near the train and bus station, which was a big help when the snow was too deep to drive the automobile. We were tolerating the cramped conditions. Our daughter was six years old and there was no place for her to have her friends in to play, except for a small area in the living room. Most of the time the children would play games in the hallway, when the superintendent was away. They could get very noisy at times. Then the neighbors would complain. We decided to buy a house, but on my salary of $52.00 per week it was difficult to find one we could afford. A small house about two blocks from the apartment house came on the market for $9,000.00. I liked it, but we took too much time to make up our minds and it was sold to someone else who had acted quickly. We exhausted ourselves running all over the town looking for a house and finally came to the reality that we could not find one that we could afford.

If we used the forty-four hundred dollars for a down payment on an existing house, we would not have any reserve in case of an emergency. We didn't give up. I said, "I can build a house with my own two hands. I will find a building lot and, by building it myself, it will not cost as much as buying a resale house." My wife was dubious about my undertaking such a big task. I assured her that I could do it. FAMOUS WORDS OF INEXPERIENCE.

The first item on the agenda was to find a lot on which to build, at a price that we could afford. Most of the people in the upper income salary brackets were gravitating to the country, about ten miles away. I discovered the building lots were plentiful, but the prices had been driven up by the large number of people buying in the area. I did not give up, I just kept hoping and praying that a miracle would happen. Surely there must be a building lot that we could buy at our price.

One day I was driving down the road in a town that was most prestigious and noticed a realtor's sign on a tree. The lot looked like an incline for a ski slope. It really was so steep of an incline that I wondered how anyone could get an automobile up out of there in good weather; it was too much to consider in bad weather. I decided I could leave the auto near the road and that would solve the problem. I called the realtor and asked him the price of the lot. He said, "Eighteen hundred dollars as is." But I was too late, a young fellow had a deposit on the lot contingent upon his father looking at it and his getting suitable financing to build a house on it. This time I acted quickly and was not the successful buyer. All I could do was keep looking, I reasoned, and if there was one lot in town at a reasonable price, surely there must be another one. I decided not to give up.

One day I was driving down the road and I could not believe what I saw. A sign on the building lot. BACK ON THE MARKET. I didn't take the time to call the realtor, I rushed to his office and asked him what happened. He said the boy's father told him not to try and build a house on the lot. I told the realtor I could build on it and made a cash offer of nine hundred dollars, no contingencies, all cash, close as soon as possible. The realtor said he could not call the owner with such a ridiculous offer. I told him it was a fair price for the lot. It would need a lot of work to make it usable. Also, it was seventy-five feet wide and the building ordinance was a minimum of one hundred feet for a building lot. The realtor said they had already received a variance to build on it because it was grandfather zoned before the new zoning ordinance was put into effect. I said, "That is my offer," and I demanded he call the owner. He called and the owner said, "That buyer is having a pipe dream, he is not realistic. Tell him to get lost." I had no alternative but to forget that lot and keep looking.

Several weeks passed and one day the owner of the lot called me and asked if I was still interested in the lot. I said, "At my price, yes." He said, "Do you have the nine hundred dollars in cash and can you close immediately?" I said, "Yes, and I will close as fast as the legal papers can be processed." He told me to send him a letter of agreement to purchase at nine hundred dollars and include a hundred dollars earnest money, not refundable for any reason whatsoever. I said, "Done deal."

I hired an attorney to prepare the deed, and two weeks later I was the proud owner of a building lot in the town where I wanted to live. We had a better name for it, Big Problem Lot. My troubles were just beginning. I cut down the trees where the house was to be built. There were a lot of tree stumps all over the place, but I decided to let the excavator remove them with his big bulldozer. For him it would be easy.

I made three bonfires that looked like infernos. It took several days to burn all the debris, and now I was ready for the contractor to dig a foundation area. All the houses in the area had basements, usually built of cinder or cement blocks. The blocks were laid on what is known as a footing course, which was a three foot wide and one foot thick concrete wall around the perimeter at the bottom of the basement block.

TROUBLE GALORE: The contractor called me and said we had big trouble. The excavation was to be eight feet deep. At four feet he struck a solid rock ledge. I asked him what to do about it. He said we should blast the rock with dynamite at the cost of ninety dollars per day. I asked him how many days it would take. He estimated about ten days. I said to myself, "There goes our buffer cash that was to be kept for emergencies." I told the excavator to do nothing until I had time to decide what I wanted to do about the situation. I had to solve the problem without spending money. The answer came to me. Use the rock ledge in front of the site for a footing course, build up the rear of the plot. I decided to relocate the house twelve feet closer to the road and fill in the four extra foot depth with earth from all around the area. There was a stone fence along one side of the property that could be used for fill. PROBLEM SOLVED.

Not quite, a wet weather spring opened up in the basement floor area. That would make the basement wet every time it rained. Again I had to put on the thinking cap. This one was easy. I remembered the stone fence. I would put stones over a drain tile and pipe the water under the floor, out the rear of the basement. It worked much to my advantage. A lot of people had wet basements when it rained. I had a built in drain so I had a bone dry basement floor. I even carpeted it later and made a recreation room out of the space.

It took me all summer to put in the footing course and lay the blocks. It went very slowly because I had to mix the cement and carry the blocks to the wall. I decided to lay an extra course of block in order to raise the house higher. I now had to carry the blocks up a scaffolding, which was not easy. I finally had all the blocks in place.

More trouble that I did not think of arose. I could not put the lumber onto the foundation because winter was coming and if water got into the blocks and pocketed it there, it would freeze and break the blocks and ruin the foundation. I decided to cover the blocks with tar paper and wait until springtime to start putting the lumber into place. It was a good thing to take a break because I was very tired and didn't realize it in my anxiety to get the house built. I was running out of nervous energy.

During the winter, fortune smiled on me. On my factory job I was making blue prints for the machine parts and I had access to the printing equipment. I decided to make uni-part blueprints for every part of the house, that way I would not have to do any figuring on the construction of the house. I could nail the wood together on the floor and just stand it up and attach it to the adjacent part. Almost like a youngster's erector toy set. It worked very well and sped up the erection of the house. I could saw everything to length without having to measure and without trial and error fitting.

Springtime came and I ordered the lumber. They were able to unload it near to where the house would be built. I laid the sill planks on top of the cinder block and bolted them down. It seemed like a few hours and I had that portion completed. I said to myself, "This is going to be a snap." WRONG! VERY WRONG!

The main support for the floor joists had to be run from one end of the basement wall to the other side. Thirty-six feet of two by twelve planks, three of them bolted together. I could reach seven feet, but the top of the foundation was nine feet from the floor. The planks were twelve feet long and, I found out, very heavy. BIG PROBLEM. I thought about it for a minute and said, "Build a tripod and lay the planks on to the top of it." Problem solved. It took almost a day to get this portion done. Now I realized it would not be so easy and would not go so fast.

Laying the floor sills was easy. All I had to do was to follow the blueprint and put the planks into place. They didn't have to be nailed at this time, so again Speedy was encouraged by the results of this operation. The sub-flooring was also very easy. All I had to do was throw a lot of the tongue and groove random length lumber onto the joists, nail them in place and trim the edges around the outside perimeter and around the stairwell to the basement.

Now the moment of truth came, cutting the first floor studs to the proper length. I was a little apprehensive about whether I had specified the correct length measurement. I laid a stop piece of two by four lumber on to the sub-floor and nervously cut about a hundred pieces all at once. I was glad I had not made a mistake because it would have put a dent into my budget if I had been wrong.

I selected the blueprint for the north east wall, then laid the lumber into place and nailed it together. The nailing was easy. Everything was right there on the floor. I got a thrill that almost brought tears to my eyes when I stood the frame work up and braced it so it would not fall. I did the same with the south east wall and attached it to the first wall. At this point I rechecked my measurements and found them correct. I could now look out through the window and door openings and get a view from the inside out. Our first house was beginning to become reality and I was awe stricken. I just sort of believed it would not happen, but there it was, right in front of me. I continued the framing by laying the lumber onto the floor and nailing it into place.

It really went up very quickly and easily. My pre-planning was paying off.

The second floor was a little more complex, but it fell into place. I had to use a tripod arrangement to hold the roof rafters in place until I could securely nail them. It went well and was not too difficult.

Putting on the roof sheathing was a little dangerous because the front of the roof was steep. The rear portion was not so steep, so I put that on first. Then I had something to stand on. I completed the sheathing and covered the entire roof with a tar paper called roofing felt. It suddenly dawned on me that the house was under roof. Again I had that good feeling. This time it was like the cat that ate the canary. I would be able to work in all kinds of weather.

I installed the windows and doors. I couldn't believe that I was not having more problems. The man came and plastered the walls and ceilings. The inside of the house now looked like that of a real house. I put the clapboard siding onto the outside of the house. I painted the siding with the first coat while I had the scaffold up. It sped up the completion of the outside of the house. The inside plaster dried and I put on a coat of dark green paint in order not to have to do a second coat until we were in the house. It was to become "the awful green." It was dismal but we had to live with it for a while.

The autumn leaves had fallen and the nights were getting cold. The house had to be heated in order to keep the plumbing from freeze damage. I had the electricity connected and turned the oil burner furnace on. It felt good and gave the house the air of a home. I installed the roofing material and tacked inexpensive floor linoleum onto the sub-floor to keep the cold air from blowing up through the floor. I had the overhead garage door installed, but did not have money for the small basement door to the outside. I took crate lumber from the factory, made a door and painted it the same color as the house. In fact, it didn't look bad.

Besides it was in the rear of the house.

November 12, 1950: The big day had come. We moved into the house, sat down by the fireplace and thanked God for letting us have it.

We had two bedrooms that we could use, one of the bedrooms had the hardwood flooring and window trim stored in it. We had a living room, dining room, eat in kitchen and two full bathrooms. What a change from our cramped apartment living. We did not have much furniture, but we visited house furnishing sales and picked up some very nice, old furniture at a low price.

One of my co-workers was retiring and he sold us a complete antique dining room set which needed repairing. It had a large table, six chairs, a corner cabinet and a buffet. It sure helped the appearance of a sparsely furnished house. I repaired it and sold it thirty years later for one thousand dollars.

By the end of our first year in the house it was pretty well furnished. By the end of the second year we had the flooring laid and the window trim completed. The big bonus was the Heatolator fireplace; it was a unit made of steel that fit into the usual fireplace opening. A good wood fire in it would heat the whole house. It came in handy many times when the ice and snow broke the power lines. Then there would be no electricity and no heat because the oil burner needed electricity to operate it. We would stay up late at night and keep logs on the fire until the wee hours of the morning. Then we could get a few hours sleep before the fire went out.

Lady luck smiled on us again. We needed to complete the front yard and driveway. The good old stone fence was right there to save us. I put the stones on the driveway, broke them into small pieces and covered them with earth as a binder. The remainder of the stones we put into the front yard and I brought fill earth to fill in the four foot hole caused by the rock ledge problem. We sowed grass seed and had a nice lawn. Thirty-two years later we sold the house for over four times what it cost to build, of course inflation was the big factor in the price increase.

We took the money and built a real nice ranch style house in Winter Park, Florida, where we live today. I called our first house PPPP—Planning, Pain, Patience and Perseverance.

The Gold
Doorknob
Mystery

The year was 1960. I was twenty-one years of age, and after many months of seeking gainful employment, I was successful in finding full-time employment in a large factory as supervisor of assembly, quality control and electrical testing.

The factory's main products were special ornamental doors, unique windows and unusual style cabinets. Most of the knobs, handles and assembly hardware were made of gold and silver. The factory catered to the mansion owners, or as they say, the rich and famous. The company was well known worldwide for producing a first class product at a fair price.

The factory operated on a cost plus basis. This gave the purchasers the opportunity to make changes without issuing a new contract.

The company employed about two hundred very capable employees that were trustworthy. There was seldom a discrepancy in the raw material inventory, and if there was it was negligible. If any of the material was mislaid or stolen, it could be costly and time consuming to replace.

I had the honor of being one of the Pass Issuers. Everything that came into or went out of the factory had to have a Pass Certificate issued in duplicate and attached to it. The security guard would verify and execute the directions, which we wrote onto the certificate. He would initial the certificate and send one copy to the accounting department. The other copy would stay with the material and be sent to accounting when the material was shipped. It served as a constant inventory record and kept a check on the Pass Signer. It was a procedure I instituted in order to keep a tight security check on everyone, including me. It also served as a material location record. All special and very valuable material received would be inspected for quality and quantity, then put into a security room, which we referred to as "the vault." There were three persons that had keys to the vault—the owner of the factory, the security guard, and I. No one else was allowed to enter the vault without close supervision as to what was being removed. There were no exceptions.

I'd had the trust and respect of my employer for the past fifteen years. Everything was running along very smoothly. The control system was doing its job and there was very little to do but the routine procedure of getting the job done and shipped on time.

I suppose there is no process or venture that is perfect. It finally happened to us. BIG TROUBLE. We had completed the manufacturing of a large order for an oil magnate's mansion and were ready to prepare the items for shipping. Everything was accounted for except one solid gold doorknob. This caused a lot of trouble because we had an international shipping permit and could not do a partial shipment. I had personally inspected the twenty gold doorknobs when they were received. They were as per order. I wrapped them, individually in tissue paper, and stored them in the vault.

The factory owner took the position that perhaps we had only received nineteen. I said that was absolutely not so. I had carefully counted twenty knobs. We had received twenty of them, and I would bet my life on it. The fact that he questioned me made me suspicious of him. But why would he steal something as important as a gold doorknob?

We didn't question the security guard because he would not have been interested in a gold knob. He was a most trusted employee, and so loyal he would have reported his mother for stealing a nickel. He checked everyone through a metal detector as they entered or left the factory. I offered myself and belongings to be searched if they so desired. The factory manager said he was sure that I did not steal it. He said my integrity was beyond questioning. Now the mystery intensified.

The vault was searched from top to bottom, no knob. The factory owner called the vendor that had made the gold doorknob and asked how quickly he could furnish a replacement knob. He said he had enough of the gold to match the original shipment and he could deliver it to us within a few days. What a relief that was.

All went well, and the order from our factory went out on time, complete. We wrapped the gold knobs in a protective material, placed them into a security box and insured them—twenty of them, verified by the three pass signers. What a relief to see that shipment for the last time.

The missing gold doorknob incident played on my mind. How was it taken from tight security? Perhaps someone had picked the lock. I could not believe that either. It was a double deadlock, triple bolt lock that was impossible to spring open. I kept searching, in vain, hoping to find the knob. Its disappearance really bothered me. I kept thinking of what my father had taught me. He said, "Hunger and thirst will be forgotten, but if you lie or steal you have to live the remainder of your life with it on your conscience." I never forgot that, but how could I get anyone to be absolutely certain that I was not guilty.

The issue was forgotten as far as the factory owner was concerned. In fact, it was not mentioned again. They say, "Time and tide heals all wounds," or as I like to put it, "Wounds all heels." This was to happen years later to the guilty one. Or at least he was to be found out.

The factory in New Jersey had been closed and the building had been sold. Our factory had been moved to New York. In the process of moving, the knob did not show up. It had apparently just vanished.

I was put in charge of the new factory in New York. I

was given total authority to do whatever was necessary to continue the manufacturing process. No one ever questioned my integrity. No such incident had occurred since the missing knob fracas.

One day, I received a telephone call from the old security guard. He wanted me to stop by and repair his Philco console radio, which had a peculiar defect. Sometimes it would play, and other times it was as dead as a doornail. If you connected the test equipment to it, it would play very well until the next time you wanted to listen to it. I was a graduate radio technician and had advanced training in circuitry and theory. I had repaired many radios with the same defect and it only took a fifteen cent capacitor to fix it. Advanced electronics was my hobby.

We talked about old times and he gave me a big glass of ice cold lemonade. He asked me how much he owed me for the repair and I told him it was a favor. I didn't want any pay for fixing it. I thanked him for the lemonade and said, "I must be getting on the road to home."

I asked him if I could use the lavatory. He said, "It is down the hall, second door on the right." When I had finished, I washed my hands and dried them on a towel that hung from a nail on the back of the lavatory door. A peculiar feeling came over me, like something had upset my equilibrium. Why did this strange feeling come over me? I was concerned about my well being.

Something was very wrong. I stood still for a moment and it was like a bolt from out of the blue. There was the gold doorknob on the inside of the tenement house lavatory. I stared at it. I was dumbfounded! I said to myself, "THE GOLD DOORKNOB. IT CAN'T BE. BUT THERE IT IS. HE WOULDN'T STEAL IT. BUT YES, HE DID."

I decided to say nothing to him, to go my way and take time to decide what to do about it. I thanked him for the lemonade and said, "Enjoy your radio."

On the way home I kept thinking about what to do. My

wife was a member of the Grand Jury Association. I thought she would be able to give me good advice. She said it was up to me and my conscience. What could I profit from reporting it to the police in order to let the owner of the factory know I did not steal it? The factory owner at the time of the theft had died several years ago. The guard was an old man and he would go to jail and probably pay a huge fine. I thought of the disgrace it would bring for his children and grandchildren to find out Grandpa was a dishonest guard. In fact, he was a thief, worse than a thief. He was paid to protect the property.

I doubt if he knew the value of the knob or if he even knows today that it is probably worth thousands of dollars. It had never occurred to us to question him about the missing knob. He had nothing to do with manufacturing.

In retrospect, it would have been prudent to let him know about the situation it created. I decided to just forget it. It wasn't an easy decision to make. I was very angry. He had put me in a very embarrassing position. It took years to get it off my mind.

It has been thirty-six years since I retired from the factory, with honor and a good pension. This is the first time I have told anyone about the incident except my wife and daughter. I am glad they know the truth.

FOOD FOR THOUGHT . . . I am satisfied with my decision. What would you do in a situation like this?

Our Cayman
Islands Vacation

The year was 1986.

We sold our three houses, closed our commercial real estate business and our flying club with two airplanes, all of which were in New Jersey. We retired and moved into our new house in Winter Park, Florida. The house was built to our specifications and the contractor did a magnificent job of making certain that everything was as ordered. All we had to do to make the house livable was hang pictures and have window curtains installed.

Boredom soon set in. Suddenly we had nothing to do. I planted a vegetable garden and some shrubbery, just to keep from going bananas. The transition from working fourteen hours a day to doing nothing was getting to us.

My wife and I decided to build a large flea market in East Orlando, Florida. Of course, we would require about three million dollars to complete the project. We heard the Grand Cayman Islands were a money capitol. Excellent! We could vacation and look for the money at the same time.

The wife of one of our former employees had opened a travel agency in Florida. I telephoned her and made arrangements for this trip. Our daughter drove us to the Orlando International Airport. I presented our tickets to the airline ticket clerk. She said, "Tampa is only a twenty-four minute trip, why are you flying instead of driving?" She asked if this was our first airplane experience. I said that we were seasoned travelers and this is the first of two flights this morning. I explained that we were continuing on to the Grand Cayman Islands on Cayman Air. She made my day be saying, "How exciting!" and she mentioned that she wished she could go along.

She looked over the seating availability and said, "How would you like to ride in the first class seats, no extra charge." I thanked her and we were seated among the elite. As soon as we were airborne, the stewardess brought us a newspaper and asked which cocktail we preferred. Not being a drinker, I could only think of a Manhattan, whatever that was. She was back in a flash with the drinks and a breakfast tray. She asked, "Regular or decaffeinated coffee?" We said, "Regular." Again, within a minute she was back with the drink.

By now, I had both hands full and I spilled the coffee down the front of my shirt and trousers. The coffee was not very hot, but I spent the remainder of the flight to Tampa trying to get my clothing as dry as possible. I used a lot of napkins and managed to get most of the moisture out.

We arrived at Tampa Airport at the east end of the terminal, Cayman Air Gate was at the west end. As I walked, I held my carry-on in front of me so the people would not think that Gramps didn't make it to the privy in time.

The cover up worked and we were seated on Cayman Air Number 282. It was a smooth flight, and we were served a very good breakfast. This time I drank the coffee. It's amazing how quickly we learn to drink it and not spill it all over ourselves.

Upon arrival in the Caymans I started taking photographs. I was trying to film the customs building and the Cayman Island welcome sign. I got off the customs limits and an officer reminded me that I had to go through customs before I went onto Cayman territory.

I was excited about being in what I was told is a tropical paradise. I learned later the brochures and reality were far apart. More about that later in the story.

The Customs Officer directed me to the proper entrance line for inspection in order to be cleared into the island. I was excited about being able to enjoy the vacation and trying to arrange the loan. At last through customs, I called a taxi and proudly directed him to take us to the Cayman Islander

Motel. I noticed a peculiar look on his face when I mentioned that motel. About twenty minutes later I got the reason for his expression. We arrived at the motel and I went into the registration office. I expected the interior of the motel to have some decor like what I perceived would be a tropical palace. Surprise!!! It was the Cayman version of a run-down American motel of days gone by. I asked the bellhop to tell me about the facility. He said, "You will like it. It has a lot of island charm and entertainment."

Dinner time was approaching and I looked around for the restaurant their brochure mentioned. The travel agent had also informed us that there was one. I finally gave up trying to locate it and asked the bellhop to direct me. He said, "Go along the south side of the building, there is a screened window, ring the buzzer and a waitress will take your order and serve you, picnic style."

The thought of being fed through a window didn't excite me. While she was taking our order, I sneaked a peek at the interior of the kitchen. It looked like the aftermath of a tornado, but it was clean. Within a reasonably short time she handed us our food on a tray and said the beverages would be right over there in the vending machines. Also, there was a water fountain, and she said we could help ourselves.

Another surprise! The food was good and plentiful. We ate on picnic benches, which were also very clean. There were no flies or bugs to annoy us. They must have sprayed to keep them away. It turned out to be a very good dining experience and we had breakfast there. They had excellent choices on the menu. I suppose we especially enjoyed it because it was the closest. The other restaurant was a half mile up the road and it was raining.

A big surprise. There was a sixteen percent island tax added to the bill for the food. It was not too expensive even with the server's gratuity. The money rate of exchange was one twenty Cayman to one U. S. dollar. That helped take the sting out of it. We decided to inspect our room very carefully to learn of any surprises, if any existed.

I looked at the window air conditioner, which looked like a rusty something with three knobs on it. I expected it to be inefficient and noisy. I carefully turned it to the ON position and was treated to a blast of cold air. It was as quiet as the boss when you asked for an increase in salary, or a day off with pay. So far, so good.

I turned the television on and it worked perfectly. My wife said that everything was going so well that it ruined my day. I couldn't find anything to complain about. She is a sweet little lady and she knows me. Some day I will hide her beer money. Ha Ha Ha.

It was now about six thirty in the evening and we were wondering where was the entertainment that was to be so wonderful. There was no entertainment building or room. Just a liquor bar along side the motel covered with a corrugated tin roof. There were lots of bar stools and chaise lounges, but no bartender in sight. I thought, how would you get a drink? The thought occurred to me that you would have to ring the buzzer by the food window. Not so, about seven o'clock the barmaids showed up and opened the security grating that was protecting the liquor bottles. The tourists started to fill the seats and the girls started to serve the drinks. A lot of natives arrived with their musical instruments and sang and drank and drank and sang. The island music was very good. One of the musicians played a steel drum and he was the life of the party. There was so much energy that it got you into the mood to join in the fun. I got caught up in the (oh well, confession is good for whatever) drinking. I had a few nip and tuck cocktails. The kind that after a few nips, and they tuck you in for the night. WOW! ! What an evening! We went for a swim in the big pool where the water was about ninety degrees Fahrenheit. The air was warm and we sat around for an hour just trying to settle down from all the celebration.

We had a good night's sleep. The beds were clean and comfortable.

The next morning, we decided to walk to Georgetown. A very impressive town of tall buildings, sort of like Wall Street, with banks and money lending institutions everywhere. There was no massive advertising, just the company names in the usual gold letters, very low key. We walked around for a while and arrived at the museum, which was very interesting.

We picked up a folder that advertised a submarine dive ride for fifty-dollars U.S. We decided to go for it. They took us down fifty feet to where the big sea life is. The Captain explained the types of fish and sea monsters. We saw the remains of a ship that had sunk many years before. Each passenger had his or her own seat and port hole, so the ride was comfortable. The Caymans are know worldwide as a haven for snorkelers.

It was now lunch time. We looked all over for a restaurant. The only eating place we found in Georgetown was an ice cream parlor. We enjoyed a big cone of excellent quality ice cream. We asked some tourists if they had found some place to eat. They said there was a Burger King up the road a short distance, and we went there. It was a wooden shack set on wood pilings at the edge of the beach. Very rustic, but it was a Burger King and we enjoyed the low cost food.

The island is famous for a seven mile white sand beach. We decided to walk the beach instead of walking the road back to our motel, there was little else to do anyway. Within a short distance, we saw the Holiday Inn, right on the beach. By now we were getting thirsty and decided to enjoy one of their what they called "Tropical Coolers." We gulped it instead of sipping, and it put the cooler on to us. The chaise lounge served as a recovery facility.

We'd had enough of the beach walk. The road was nearby, so we decided to investigate what was up the road.

We went up a wide, beautifully landscaped driveway to see what was in the huge building. A guard dressed in a military uniform asked with whom did we have an appointment. I said we were just exploring the island and were curious what the building contained. He said it was the Governor's mansion. I jokingly said he probably wouldn't be interested in seeing me anyway. I excused myself and went back out to the main highway.

The next building we saw was the Hyatt Regency Hotel. It was a real tropical showplace on the south side of the island by the ocean. We went into the dining room and splurged on a gourmet lunch, fifty-dollars Cayman money, plus the infamous sixteen percent, plus tip.

I became a little ritzy with all the above average amenities, and impressed with all the people we saw. I said to my wife, "Let's check out of Lower Slabovia and stay at the Regency, after all, this is a business trip and a well earned vacation." I asked the desk clerk for a rate chart, he handed me one and informed me that there would not be a vacancy for at least three days. I was shocked at the price of a standard room, $265.00 plus tax, and bellhop gratuity of ten percent a day. Deluxe suites were priced at figures beyond my wildest imagination, average dinners were around a hundred dollars, plus.

Lower Slabovia never looked so good.

On the way back to the motel we saw several restaurants with their bill-of-fares on placards in the windows. Their prices were also in the astronomical range. We were lucky, we found a Mexican Restaurant that also served good American type food at very reasonable prices. Dinner for two, including tax and gratuity, would be about thirty dollars. They also served big sandwiches and beverages for under six dollars, Cayman money.

Back at the motel, we enjoyed a relaxing evening, had a window snack and called it a day. There was no entertainment; that was only on Friday evenings. Too bad, it was real good excitement.

Sunday morning we decided to start out early, have breakfast at Burger King and go to church. The church in Georgetown is an all denominational sanctuary. We went in and sat in large wooden pews on the left hand side of the aisle. A very distinguished gentleman came over to where we were sitting and said, "Follow me." On the way to seats on the right side of the aisle, he explained that seats on the left side were for poor people. He said we looked affluent and asked if we were there on business or pleasure. I said the answer was both; we were on vacation and we were there to try to arrange a three million dollar U.S. loan to finance the erection and start up operation funds for a flea market in East Orlando, Florida. He asked me for my proforma and I had a copy for his perusal.

The church service began and we listened to a good sermon and an excellent large choir. After church, we thanked our new found acquaintance and started to walk up the road. It started to rain and we opened our umbrellas. A few hundred feet from the church our new found friends stopped and asked if they could drive us to the motel. I said that would be much appreciated. I explained that we did not rent an auto due to the driving on the left hand side of the road. I informed them we were staying at the Cayman Islander. I suppose his wife knew of the limited eating facilities there because she suggested we have lunch at their house and by then, she said, the rain probably would have stopped.

Their house was a real tropical residence. Shrubbery and vines were almost covering the house, flower gardens were everywhere. While his wife was preparing the food, her husband and I discussed my request for the loan. He asked how much of our money I planned to invest as a down payment. I said I wanted to borrow the entire amount. He said he had never heard of such an arrangement. I told him my contribution to the project was to design, build and operate the market. Collect all the money and deposit it in his bank. The operation would net over three thousand dollars a week and I would give them forty percent of the net income, which would be more than the maximum interest rate allowed. It was a high profit venture. I offered to let them hold first paper to the entire equity in the market. He said it was good of me to let them have title to their investment. He apologized and said he meant that jokingly. He meant no offense, but he just had to say it. He thought about my request for a few minutes and perused my proforma. He said, "You know, it doesn't sound too bad, all things considered." He agreed to present it to his money cartel within the next few days. He said because I was a building contractor, perhaps I could help him with building an in-ground swimming pool. It was easy to advise him, especially about covering the pool deck with a material called "cool-decking," a porous material that does not get hot when exposed to the sun. He was surprised to learn of the material. It was not available on the island, so I arranged to have it shipped to him. We had a gourmet lunch and the sun came out.

We walked back to Lower Slabovia, as we referred to the motel. We spent the remainder of the day swimming, relaxing on the chaise lounges, and watching television.

Monday, The Day of Thrills!

We decided to take the municipal public bus to the east end of the island. We were at the extreme west end. The fare for the twenty-two mile round trip was four dollars per person. The semi-improved road ran along the south side of the island. The bus was a rickety old vehicle with no air conditioning. Windows that were half way open helped some, but there were no screens. The wood seats had no cushions.

We got onto the bus at Georgetown and the driver headed east. The water was splashing from potholes in the road. It had rained the night before. The wind was blowing from the rapid travel of the bus to a point where it was almost impossible to keep our eyes open. About a mile up the road, the bus stopped to take on passengers with their bags of groceries. They stashed their bags of goodies anywhere they could find room. After another few miles, there was a repeat performance of shoppers boarding the bus. Then it was away we go again, water splashing, and the air buffeting us. The unbelievable thing was that the bus driver delivered the groceries to the people's houses, which were miles off the main road. The reason for that extra is later in the story.

About ten miles into the trip, the driver stopped and picked up a petite black teenager. She sat in front of us and we had a pleasant chat with her. A white man of about fifty-years of age boarded the bus and sat in a seat across the aisle from us. He started to use abusive language toward her. He became real obnoxious and kept making unkind remarks to the girl. I asked her if she had trouble with him previously. She said she had never seen him before today. She kept twisting the handle on her handbag like she was very nervous. The fellow became very offensive and the bus driver stopped the bus, pointed his finger at him and said, "You are out of here." He got off the bus without saying a word. We found out later that the bus drivers are also sworn-in police officers.

I said to the young lady, "You were quite nervous. I saw you twisting the handle of your handbag." She said she was not afraid of him and showed me an ice pick with a six inch spike, which she had unrolled from the handle of her handbag. She said if he had attacked her, she would have defended herself, probably killing him. The bus driver did not see the weapon.

Rolling Along Again . . .

The bus driver informed us he was stopping at a little country store a few miles up the road. It was not a bus stop and he ordered everyone not to get off the bus. If we wanted anything, he would get it for us. There was a big Pepsi sign hanging out over the front of the store. Many of us had ice cold drinks. One of the passengers said this will be a twenty minute stop because the bus driver's girlfriend lived there. We were spared that problem. He and his girlfriend, with her baby, came out within a few minutes and got on the bus. The girl and her baby sat on a ledge in back of the windshield, which was a narrow board above the instruments and gauges. Americans refer to this area as the instrument panel. The girl and the driver had a pleasant conversation. I don't see how she sat up there, but she did, and she held the baby beside her. They say love will find a way.

Rolling Along Again . . .

By now, the sun was high and it was very warm on the bus. The driver, jokingly said, "If you think it is hot here, it is going to get hotter, we will be in Hell within a few minutes." Then he explained that there is a small town just ahead named Hell, after its founder. There is a card shop and post office. "You will be able to mail your friends a card and tell them you went to Hell and back," he joked. The land surface was made of grey and black protruding rocks, which looked awful.

We had a ten minute stop, then the driver took us to the turtle farm. A guide took us around and explained how they raise turtles for food and pets. The turtles range from the size of a silver dollar to six hundred pounds. They are separated in holding and growing tanks. There were hundreds of turtles to see. One of the outstanding things about raising turtles is they put the babies into an inclined box so they learn to climb. It strengthens their legs through exercise.

When we got back on the bus, there were only six passengers that boarded for the return trip. The driver said he was going to give us an extra treat. He was not supposed to drive to the extreme east end of the island where the rich people had their mansions, but he would take us there anyway. It was worth seeing how the very rich live. I became a little apprehensive about the driver's intentions. Why was he leaving the designated bus route? I had no defensive weapon. The girl with the ice pick had gotten off the bus. I looked around for anything I could find to protect me and my wife if we were subjected to any harm. I couldn't find anything. I decided to act swiftly if we were attacked. The bus driver was pleasant, but he would not have broken the top off an I.Q. registering scale.

It turned out alright. He said he was giving us a little extra sightseeing because his income, in part, relied on grateful passenger gratuities. I was relieved to learn we were not going for our last ride. The thought occurred to me that his girlfriend might be an accomplice to holding us up, and they had the advantage.

The trip back to Georgetown was uneventful and we were anxious to get into that hot water swimming pool.

Tuesday . . .

We were glad to be back on Cayman Air heading for Florida, U.S.A. The fact that the travel agent didn't know too much about the island contributed to a very exciting vacation and business trip.

I received a Christmas card from the money man, but there was no mention of my three million dollar dilemma.

I will always remember the Lower Slabovia jamboree.